The UFO Chronicles |

District of Columbia

JUSTIN SNEAD

Paint Creek Press

Disclaimer:
This is a work of fiction. None of the people or events depicted in these pages are intended to represent historical reality, though each story contains a small number of fictionalized representations of historical events (see *Author's Note* for more details). None of the various depictions of the UFO occupants in this collection ought to be interpreted as the truth behind who or what is sending the UFOs—except for the one that, in the fullness of time, turns out to be correct. That one was intentional.

Other books by the author:

*UFO Disclosure Yearbook Series: A Reference Guide, Oral History, and Commentary
on the year in UFO Disclosure*

- The UFO Disclosure Yearbook | 2023 *(available now)*
- The UFO Disclosure Yearbook | 2024 *(coming in 2025)*

THE UFO CHRONICLES | DISTRICT OF COLUMBIA

For my husband, whose love and support keeps me from venturing too far down the rabbit hole. And for my seven-year-old daughter, who is a better storyteller than me.

CONTENTS

—Oral History Project description, from the Department of Homeland Security Proposed Special Access Program for the Advanced Technology Threat Program, codenamed *Kona Blue*, 2011 (classified Top Secret until 2023)

UNCLASSIFIED

~~TOP SECRET//KONA BLUE//NOFORN~~
~~HANDLE VIA SPECIAL ACCESS CHANNELS ONLY~~

Over past decades a number of high-level individuals in the military, intelligence, and even political sectors of our government have had various level of exposure/access to this subject area. This has included agency directors, members of the JCS and very senior individuals in the Executive Branch. To this can be added certain foreign heads of state, as well as select members of the government contractor community in the electronics and aerospace sectors. Oral histories from individuals of the caliber referenced above are critical to this mission.

- Data collection from an already identified and calibrated list of retired, previously highly placed government, armed services, contractor and intelligence community individuals. The oral history project will include gathering all information pertaining to the *location* of advanced aerospace technology and biological samples, including records, files, reports, photographs, as well as physical samples.

—Toni Morrison, *Unspeakable Things Unspoken: The Afro-American Presence in American Literature*, 1988

We can agree, I think, that invisible things are not necessarily "not-there"; that a void may be empty but not be a vacuum. In addition, certain absences are so stressed, so ornate, so planned, they call attention to themselves; arrest us with intentionality and purpose, like neighborhoods that are defined by the population held away from them. …The spectacularly interesting question is "What intellectual feats had to be performed by the author or his critic to erase me from a society seething with my presence, and what effect has that performance had on the work?" What are the strategies of escape from knowledge? Of willful oblivion?

| 1 |

Bucket of Piss

The UFO landed on the White House lawn at 3:47 AM on September 4th. It was shaped like two convex discs pressed together, tapering to a sharp edge, perfectly symmetrical. It was all one color, a dull light gray, except for a shallow dome on its top, which was translucent white with a shimmer, like a mound of fresh snow glinting in sunlight. There were no other features or markings. The dimensions were forty feet in diameter, fifteen feet from the lowest point of the ventral side to the top of the dome, making it more sleek than bulbous. These numbers had to be estimated visually since every sensor beam that was aimed at it warped around the hull. No one who saw the UFO needed that kind of data to satisfy their curiosity. It looked exactly like what everyone who had ever joked about a flying saucer landing on the White House lawn imagined that it would look like.

The above description fits what people saw in the full sun of that clear blue day. At 3:47 AM it was like a shadow.

No one saw it land. Moving slow, it descended straight down to its resting position on the South Lawn, among the trees between the fountain and the vegetable garden, closer to the fence and tourist stands on E Street than the building itself. For every part of this maneuver the craft was completely silent. It was not picked up by radar, nor did it set off any perimeter alarms. No one even knew it was there for twenty-six minutes.

When Secret Service agents in the observation deck above the Truman balcony noticed the odd shape, they all agreed it was probably temporary construction for the upcoming holiday weekend, and they began leafing through reports to confirm. Agents could often never decide if the set dressing of the political shop's photo ops were above their pay grade or below it, but they were clear that it was not possible for them to care less about such things. That weekend there was to be a congressional cookout, a final fantasia of flesh pressing and brandy sipping to lock up the last recalcitrant votes for the President's entitlement reform bill.

Since the agents could not recall whether or not the structure was there when they came on shift, the senior agent's first call was to the White House Social Secretary. After fumbling the clattering phone off her nightstand, she was slow to understand what the gruff voice was asking, but was able to mumble that the stage was not scheduled to be erected until that afternoon.

"Any kiddie rides?" the agent asked. "Like those UFO-shaped spinning things they have at carnivals?"

"Um... what?" the Social Secretary replied.

It was not until a bleary-eyed staffer, summoned to a pre-dawn stroll by the cries of the President's new goldendoodle puppy, noticed the thing was floating eight feet above the grass that the entire compound was evacuated.

Some fled through the north gates and ran up Pennsylvania Avenue. Most inhabitants of the building dropped into the tunnels. The entire White House complex emptied like a flushed toilet.

Initially the pilot of Air Force One was told to prepare for continuous flight maneuvers, and refueling tankers were ordered to taxi on various runways across the country. Then the Secretary of the Air Force suggested, given the nature of the situation, it might be more prudent to get out of the sky. The President, his wife, and the goldendoodle were deep underground at NORAD by mid-morning.

He was still on the plane when he convened the first video conference with his national security team. There were eleven boxes on the screen. The two in the top row were the President and his long-serving White House Chief of Staff, Bob Xenakis. In the second row were the Directors of National Intelligence, CIA and Homeland Security, and the Secretary of Defense. Below them were the Chairman of the Joint Chiefs, and the Secretaries of the Army, Navy and Air Force. In the bottom square live video of the UFO cycled every ten seconds from different security cameras.

BEGIN TRANSCRIPT

POTUS: Okay….[voices off screen] Which one of you is going to tell me what in God's name this thing is?

WHCoS: I think we all know the answer to that one, Mr. President.

POTUS: Bobby, pipe down. Let's hear from the experts first please.

WHCoS: Of course, sir. All right everyone, what have you got?…. Chairman?

CJC: Uh… [shuffling papers] We're still waiting on intel, Mr. President.

DNI: Mr. President, if I may… I think the straight answer is we don't know yet.

CIA: It could be a hoax.

POTUS: Why do you say that, Harriet?

CIA: The UFO wing-nut community, a portion of them are fanatical. They are obsessives. Giving us a good scare like this--

WHCoS: The thing is floating.

CIA: Says the dog walker. Who saw it in the dark before sun up. It's not inconceivable that we ran out of there because of an inflatable tethered to the trees.

POTUS: And the Secret Service...?

DNI: We can't rule out human error. Somebody taking a nap, refilling their coffee. Even if the thing did land, there is equipment failure. Radar is not an exact science.

WHCoS: Come on guys. We know what it is.

POTUS: Bobby... Who controls the ground? Why aren't we crawling all over this thing?

SECARMY: That'd be us, sir. [shuffling papers] We're waiting on medical clearance. There's concern about radiation. ... I've seen reports of similar circumstances where the thing has emitted radiation, and there have been health effects...

POTUS: What do you mean reports? What reports?

SECARMY: Reports of similar circumstances.

POTUS: Hold on a damn minute.... You're saying these things are real?

SECARMY: uh... Mr. President... That's, uh... That is a DNI question. We like to defer to their analytic tradecraft standards for judgements such as that.

DNI: Well...

POTUS: Do not talk to me like I am one of your bootlickers in the press.

SECARMY: --But what I was about to say... I should probably say... uh... A report came across my desk... oh, about six to eight weeks ago of a similar object to, you know, to what we see at the White House, it was buzzing around Naval Submarine Base in King's Bay, Georgia. Wasn't corroborated.

WHCoS: Really? Wow. Ok. Everyone on this call knows that is where we put the nukes on subs, right?

SECNAV: I should probably cough up too, sir. This past June, a vehicle fitting this description trailed the John C. Stennis for about an hour and then did a... a kind of a touch-and-go maneuver on the foredeck.

POTUS: You're telling me a UFO, maybe this same UFO, landed on one of our aircraft carriers?

SECNAV: It didn't land, sir. Hovered about 10 feet off the deck and then moved off.

POTUS: Just like this thing is hovering 10 feet over my wife's cucumbers?

SECNAV: Yes sir.

POTUS: And no one knows about this?

WHCoS: Oh people know.

SECDEF: Documentary evidence was recorded by Stennis's VIPR team. Some of that was leaked to one of the wing-nut websites. We had to confirm its authenticity. But no one in the press picked it up. It stayed deep in the wing-nut... the real cuckooland part of the internet.

POTUS: Jim, and this is an honest-to-God question, what did you… You've got a nuclear reactor on the Stennis. I mean, for God's sake, you could have been boarded?

SECNAV: We were not boarded, Mr. President. The entire incident was inexplicable. Sailors don't handle that well. It's not our mission to investigate sightings of unknown or unexplained phenomena outside the context of investigating credible threats, potential threats, or potential distress in the case of search and rescue. This was deemed not a threat.

POTUS: Do we feel threatened now?

[…]

CIA: It's safe to say this is an escalation.

POTUS: An escalation of what?

WHCoS: Mr. President.

POTUS: Okay, Bobby.

WHCoS: My main job is to channel the best information to you, Mr. President, and I am failing at that right now.

POTUS: You don't say.

WHCoS: Kings Bay. The Stennis. Now D.C. This is a classic UFO wave. Sometimes there are multiple sightings in a geographic area over weeks or months. Happened in the Hudson Valley in 1983. Belgium in 1989. The Virginia Coast training area from 2013 to 2015.

POTUS: Take a breath, Bobby, and listen to me. Obviously Congress is not going to get their picnic, but I want my vote. How does this change the timetable for the entitlement reform bill? … You heard me?

WHCoS: [deep breath] There is no provision to vote remotely. They have to convene, never been done outside of the Capitol. But sir... UFOs have buzzed or landed on military compounds for decades--

POTUS: You are going to have to let these people worry about that, Bobby. Congress--

WHCoS: [agitated] Sometimes they land. Shahrokhi Air Force base outside of Tehran. Rendlesham Forest in England. Loring Air Force Base in Maine--

POTUS: The Speaker--

WHCoS: [extremely agitated] Everything depends on knowing whether they think the South Lawn is no different from any other government compound, or whether they know it's not. We have to plan for the possibility that they are here for you, sir.

POTUS: Allright get him off. Bobby, go find the Speaker of the House. Tell him to find a place to reconvene.

WHCoS: Mr. President, we need more voices in the room. All of these people on the screen, everything to them is hammers or nails. Anything else, does not compute-- [WHCoS disconnected]

POTUS: [heavy sigh] He's been a UFO nut since his congressional staffer days. Thinks there are alien bodies in a morgue under Area 51. You all need to hear me. I have been kissing ass on this entitlement bill for two years, and now I've got a three-week window in which it must pass. Then the VP and the rest of the seven dwarves start their primary debates and I am officially duck confit. I am not losing my last bill because of something out of a Saturday morning serial.

DNI: Come again, sir. Cereal? Breakfast?

POTUS: Serial. Movies. None of you ever went to the Saturday picture when you were kids? ... Forget it. [voices off screen] I'm landing. We will meet again in one hour, and I want hard facts and zero speculation.

DNI: The VP will be secure by then. Should we patch her in?

POTUS: Why the fuck would we do that? [voices off screen] Everyone just pray the damn thing flies off by then.

END TRANSCRIPT

Before the sun was up that morning, just as the D.C. evacuation orders were being formulated, Susan White, the Vice President, sat on her back patio staring into the blue light of her computer. After a long pause, paralyzed with indecision about which of the nonsensical phrases to replace with merely stultifying ones, she pushed back from the wrought iron table and let her eyes rest on the shadowy green grounds of the Naval Observatory and the wall of trees that formed the barrier between her backyard and Massachusetts Avenue. The birds were beginning their morning calls. A helicopter thrummed overhead, moving downtown. The city was waking up, which meant she only had a few minutes before she would not be able to produce a single thought for herself. She slumped lower in the chair, sipping her tea, now cold. She could not bring herself to look back at the screen.

Just read it as is, she told herself. *Power through. It doesn't matter.*

The speech was crap as usual. It was not the language but the content. She'd been giving the same type of speech in the same type of place for seven years. And they kept having the same nil effect. Yet she gave them week after week, year after year, hoping this time would be different. It was never different. The world went on unchanged as if she'd never said a word, or existed at all.

This one was a real peach too. She was going to deliver it next week in Bogotá. There would be important meetings with the President and opposition leaders, but the ostensible reason for the speech was to tout a new app developed by American college students for State Department prize money. If every citizen downloaded it onto any model smart phone, the app would help maintain peace and prosperity across their country. Just three clicks.

The real reason for the speech was to burnish her national security cred before the primary debates.

As those debates crept closer on her calendar, and the summer-long flatline that was her poll numbers continued their flat progression, Susan had begun to have inklings that she was wasting her time. In her political career she had been strapped onto more than a few rockets that imploded on the launch pad, so she knew how to sense a failure to launch. So many people in her profession lived on hope alone. The magic trick of believing their own bullshit came easy to them. Susan just did not have this ability. No matter how long she studied herself in the mirror, or stared into her own pixelated eyes in recordings of media appearances, she could not will herself to believe what she was selling. She liked to tell herself this was because she was too honest. Her staff, and especially the White House staff, thought she was too full of herself. But what was she supposed to do with an app to end civil war in Colombia? How could she elevate that? How could she be better when that is the medium?

No one appreciated that she asked these questions, so at some point after the last election she got quiet and kept her head down.

Susan had clinched genuine accomplishments on her own terms. But they felt like a lifetime ago, back in the South Carolina state house when she was just starting. Mostly she'd had lucky breaks. She was only thirty-eight when plucked into the vice presidency. She had been coasting ever since, comfortable in every way. It had been a long time since she had made an impact on any part of the real world, or left a lasting impression on any person.

In that pre-dawn stillness, a solution emerged into her thoughts fully formed, like her subconscious had been putting it together in the backroom for a while without any input from her. It was not a complicated plan. She would go through the motions for a few months before dropping out just before Christmas. She would walk away so quietly that after a news cycle or two no one would notice that she was gone. After Brad Allen's or the other guy's inauguration, she would hook up with a lobbying firm and devote herself to becoming as rich as possible until dementia hit. When Susan realized that her mind was made up, she became so giddy with relief that she laughed out loud, a high-pitched, breathy cackle.

She could disappear, become a different person. It was really this simple.

But the laughter and peace of mind fell away. She knew it would not be that easy to walk away, and even if she figured out how to pull it off, she would still be left with the same core problem. The deeper truth, which roiled beneath the surface of her thoughts during these rare quiet moments, was that Susan was wasting something much more valuable than just her time. She could not put her finger on it. She did not want to. The trick was to not allow herself many quiet moments like this. Fortunately it was interrupted by her husband, Brian Peterson, the Second Gentleman, her biggest booster, her number one voter.

He swept through the open French doors from the kitchen carrying two trays, one on each hand. Susan's breakfast was a tall glass of kale and beet juice, runny egg on buttered toast, half a grapefruit, and a fresh cup of hot tea. She consumed this in an unvarying sequence. She ate the egg toast first, pushing into her mouth with one hand while her other fingers continued to scroll or type through whatever morning work she was finishing. She gave the grapefruit her full attention, its tart sweetness the only part of the breakfast she enjoyed. Then she gulped the juice as quickly as she could get it down, and cleared her palate with sips of tea. The other tray contained the rest of her morning routine. A plate of vitamins with a glass of water. Throat spray. Shea butter. Two wigs in ziplock bags. An assortment of combs. A makeup kit. And the clipboard with Brian's daily schedule.

He was by no means her personal assistant. But it was comforting to her to have their household run as precisely as her work schedule, especially with the kids. She did not like to be managed. If having Brian help out kept staff out of the house for half an hour, it was worth it. Besides, he took to the role with gusto.

"Good morning, sweetie," he greeted, drawn out like a game show announcer. Brian was almost always chipper but never so much as when he was right out of bed. He slid the computer aside and arrayed her breakfast before her.

She mumbled her own good morning, picked up the tea and resumed her vacant stare at the trees.

Brain angled his mouth toward the phone in his shirt pocket. "Siri, play—"

Susan karate chopped the air between them. "Not yet."

"Are you okay?"

She forced a smile. "No better or worse than usual. Just another day." To prove this was not a lie she sat up and began pushing the toast into her mouth while skimming the topsheet of his clipboard. Before setting it aside to enjoy the grapefruit, she flipped through the pages underneath where the bad news was buried. Today it was a memo from her campaign manager, marked urgent. Three months of working together and they had already figured out that whenever they had a note she was not going to like it was best to deliver it through Brian.

"What's he want?"

"Small thing. Easy fix."

"What, Brian?"

"It's your waves. He wants you to try something different."

"My hair, again?"

"No, your wave. How you move your hand."

"What's wrong with my wave?"

"Well..." Brian stepped back, squared his shoulders. He raised his forearm perpendicular to his upper arm, let the hand go limp and then jiggled it on the wrist. "It kinda looks like this. The team seems to think it might be off putting."

"Off putting. Huh." Susan fell back in the chair. "What if I don't want to do this?"

"You don't have to take it personally, honey. They're just worried about the memes. That's all. Just the memes."

"No, Brian, what if I don't want to do any of this anymore?"

Brian's mouth formed a sly grin as he raised his index finger, which was his favorite gesture for when he thought he knew exactly what to do. He pried open the clip of the clipboard, reached under the papers and pulled out three rectangles of cardstock glued to popsicle sticks. Fanned out in front of his face, the first two showed two digital printouts of black-and-white photographs. They were Susan's great-grandfather and great-grandmother, South Carolina sharecroppers. The third card only had a name, Sophie. She was the wellspring of the family. Other than her name, only two facts were known. She was born in 1836 in Bladen County, almost certainly a slave.

Brian fluttered the great-grandfather card. "Look here by golly, it's Susan White. Why never in our wildest dreams—" Mercifully, he did not attempt an accent.

Susan recoiled in horror. "Oh My God. Brian. Stop."

He peeked over the cards. "We practiced this in therapy."

Susan nodded. "See, this is my fault. I did not think this all the way through. My white husband playing sock puppets with my dead, enslaved relatives. *That* is off putting."

She did not want to laugh. It would only encourage him. Her throat tightened, but the laugh came out like a bubble of hot air belching through a crust of magma. This was followed by a hiss of giggles. Brian, encouraged, joined her. Their eyes met, and they almost did not recognize the face grinning back at them. Laughing together was not something that happened very often anymore. For that one shared moment the pressure that had hardened over their marriage dissolved. After the joke was out of their system, they mustered one more bout of chuckles to keep hold of the moment.

"Not going to need these," Brian said in an imitation of a squeaky sock puppet voice, and then tossed the cards over his shoulder. But as soon as he heard the three avatars clatter on the slate his eyes tightened in a panic.

"That was insensitive," he solemnly intoned before darting after them and carefully nestling them back inside the clipboard.

They met in college. Susan did not find him impressive, but she was charmed. They laughed all the time, and they could play together, which was never an experience she'd had with a man. Whatever quality of his youth had made him merely goofy had left him by middle age, and now Susan frequently wondered if she had married an outright fool. But he was sweet, thoughtful, totally devoted, and without guile—all qualities that in her line of work outshined any fault.

Susan plunged the serrated spoon into the grapefruit. The sweetness caused a thin plaque of joy to blot out the existential gyre that was swirling open in her brain.

"I'm serious, Brian," she said, gnashing the fruit, juice on her lips. "Even if I win, somehow kneecap Brad Allen in the primary—"

"Oh we will. I'll Tonya Harding that bitch."

His earnestness, and the understanding that he would at least seriously consider it, made them both laugh one more time.

"If we do, do I want this life?"

Brian's eyes twitched. He looked to the clipboard, then the floor, then the dark wall of trees where his wife's attention kept drifting. He had used up his only strategy.

"I thought we were past these conversations," he whispered.

"Yeah, I did too."

Another helicopter passed low, just above the treetops. It was followed by three others. Susan thought this was an unusual amount of activity in the air so early in the morning. She began to worry that there was some training exercise or visiting dignitary she had forgotten about. The urge to check her daily schedule and start her day was overwhelming, but she thought it might prove fruitful to linger to the end of this conversation with her husband. When her attention returned to him, Brian had settled into the next chair at the patio table. He was talking through the techniques and strategies that he had used to get through his own midlife crisis a few years before.

Susan nodded along with the remedies to the problem he was misdiagnosing as her gaze drifted to the window into the living room that was just over his left shoulder. Her eyes stuck on the long slab of ash-gray rock that was mounted above the fireplace mantle. Centered in the rock was a dark, metallic gray fossil of a fat-bodied fish. It had a wide head with a dimple where the eye once was, some sharp teeth sticking out of the mouth, and two little hand-like fins poking down, one below the neck and the other just before the tail. It was lying in the same pose as it had flopped down and died however many hundreds of millions of years ago.

Its face, in particular the shallow eye, had always exerted a mysterious pull on Susan. She often caught herself staring into it, wondering how it could be that she felt the eye staring back at her, judging her. This had developed into an odd relationship for an art piece that she only hung because it complemented the wallpaper. She could never remember its scientific name. The fossil had been a gift from the president of Greenland.

The extinct fish always impressed the smart people at social events. Munching canapés, they would point at its anatomy and extol its evolutionary significance. It had evolved primitive lungs that could pull oxygen out of the air, but that little nub near its head made all the difference. The fins contained separate digits, complete with finger and wrist joints, that allowed its species to tug itself into the shallow rivers and mudflats where it was the biggest fish around. They would point to the little ridges in the fossilized fins, exclaiming that when this very fish dug into the mud and pulled itself onto the bank, it had helped all life on Earth begin to pull out of the water and colonize land.

Susan always joked with those smart people that whatever amazing innovation that fish and its relatives had figured out, it had not been enough. The species was extinct after all.

She developed a whole shtick about how this fish that everyone claimed was a genius was actually stupid, but this morning Susan found herself empathizing with the fat fish on her wall. It too must have thought itself pretty clever for simply walking away from all the bigger fish with sharper mouths. It was sitting pretty on the high ground, luxuriating in the warm mud. No fish had ever had it so good. But that mud would come to cover all things in its narrow world. It should have kept moving.

If by some trick of time, when it was about to close its eyes and sink away forever, it could see what the fossilized eyehole saw—its bones and scales preserved in rock hanging on some primate's living room wall—it would have kept moving. This fish needed not to just get itself up out of the mud, it needed to become something else entirely, to sprout wings and leap into the air.

Susan's eyelids, feeling heavy, shuttered her own eyes. Her head rolled on her shoulder. She tried to evoke the same vision she wished for her fish, to see the world as it would be in a hundred million years... Nothing. Even a hundred years was murky oblivion. Instead, she felt her body being covered over, buried alive. Her consciousness began slipping into a dark hole. She came out of it only when Brian finally said something that made at least partial sense.

"... and if none of that works, this is why we have kids."

Of course. The kids. They had always made the hard days bearable. Even when they were smearing spit up and shit all over her. Even when they were stretching their teenage vocabulary to the breaking point to convince her of how much she sucks. Their happiness, not hers, was her purpose and mission. It was counterintuitive that this should be comforting, but it was.

Susan and Brian were closer to the end of that mission than the beginning. Their youngest, Chase, was starting high school next week. His big sister Emma graduated last June. Susan delivered the commencement address. Emma was two decimal points from being able to share the podium with her mother as the class salutatorian, a blow that she spent the summer recovering from. Still, she got her top choice for college. She was about to begin her gap year internship working at the New York office of McKinsey. Susan did not want Emma starting freshman year at Harvard while her mother ran for president.

Both parents were soaking up these last fleeting moments of their children's childhood. They were each still innocent in their own way, but their innocence was like a loose baby tooth held in place by a thread of tissue and spot of sticky blood. Susan and Brian knew better than the children that any day now their illusions would snap and they would become untethered, fully autonomous adults reliant on no one but themselves for their own happiness. It could happen as soon as Tuesday, when Chase would walk into his first day of high school and Emma her first job in a Manhattan skyscraper.

Between now and then, both children had bit parts in the congressional cookout at the White House.

As Susan sat on the patio listening to Brian talk weepily about the two not yet fully formed adult humans who were sleeping in their beds upstairs, she wondered why her heart rate was still increasing and breath getting short. They were supposed to ward away these fears. No matter what would become of her, some part of herself would carry on in them. No matter how bad the world would get, it was impossible not to find hope in the thought that they would have their turn and that they would do better. Her children had always been water carriers for her existential dread.

What kind of world had she helped build for them? Not only was she squandering her true potential, blind to any path that led a different way, so was the entire society of which she was nominally second in command. Susan could see only two paths for her children. Emma and Chase would learn this lesson—hopefully not as late as she now was—and choose to live a life fuller than their parents had. Or they would never learn it, and stay in the mud bank. It pained Susan to think of them rejecting her so completely, setting her high on the shelf like a relic only to be taken down at holidays—which was exactly how she thought about her own parents—but she strongly suspected that they would choose the mud bank. She had not raised rebels. Not by a long shot. Neither had anyone else, based on what she knew of the other kids in their private school.

Somewhere in Brian's sheaf of clipboard papers were the notecards on which was printed the script their children were to recite to several swing-vote senators at the cookout. The plan was for them to say something cute and precocious that would help to humanize their mother, which would result in them voting in a way that would keep her from having to cast the tie-breaking vote, and also move them to say less terrible things about her on cable news. It was not going to work of course, though it had to be done. Those senators would vote how they were always going to vote and follow their own scripts. The scariest thing to Susan, now that she was in this state of mind, was that Emma and Chase were excited to do it, eager to learn how to play the game.

Brian was still talking as he cleared the table and carried the trays into the kitchen. She watched him through the wavy tunnel vision of a dream.

Maybe it was not too late, she thought. Maybe she could find those notecards and rip them up, or at least write new words on them. But she knew she could never bring herself to do that. This life had too many hooks in her. She would soldier on, cursed with the awareness that each minute accounted for on the clipboard that she allowed to waste away only brought the inevitable extinction closer. She and Brian, Emma and Chase, everyone she knew would become fossils mounted above someone else's mantle to peer out from the eyehole as the ages spun forward into a future they had no part of.

In fact, it was spinning now. The wall of trees, the patio tiles, the house all moved around her like she was on tilt-a-whirl.

She focused on Brian standing in the doorway surrounded by an aurora of inky blackness. His arm was raised, hinging at the elbow. The forearm, wrist and palm moved back and forth in a fluid sweep, like a fish flexing through the water. She wondered, *Why is he waving at me? Am I unconscious?* But then she remembered. He was modeling her new wave, the one dictated in the memo from her campaign manager.

The ingenious brain has a solution for moments such as these. The breaker short circuits and goes dark. Susan would have to spend some time in a hospital, but after that she would get to decide. Either the thing that pushed her over the edge was really nothing, or her stay in the ward would give her the socially acceptable excuse to do the impossible thing that she did not think she could do.

Brian finally realized something was wrong. "Oh my god, we're losing her. Siri, play Lady Gaga."

The voice from the phone spoke back to him. *Ok Brian, which Lady Gaga song would you like to hear?*

"It doesn't matter, Siri," he yelped into his pocket. "Born This Way."

The first beats pumped out of the speaker system. The dendrites all throughout Susan's head were nanoseconds from snapping. But it was not the song that brought her back. It was another helicopter, louder and much lower than the others. So low in fact, it landed in the backyard.

Brian checked his clipboard. There was nothing on the schedule for another two hours. "Wonderful," he chirped. "A new assignment. Where do you think he's sending you now?"

Susan knew it was not that. "Get the kids," she gasped.

As the family climbed aboard and strapped themselves into their seats, Susan knew not to ask questions. The agents would brief her when they were safe.

***

The rest of the country woke up as if into a dream.

Initial news reports indicated something—a small plane, a weather balloon—had crashed on the White House lawn. But the evacuation orders tipped off the news organizations that something much more dramatic was afoot. After sunrise, they got their first video link, and within minutes every channel and newsfeed in the world was broadcasting live video of the unmoving craft. The Army allowed a camera stand on the far side of the Ellipse, which at extreme zoom provided a grainy view of the craft's profile. The best view came from a circling military helicopter that had a crossbeam bristling with cameras and sensors. One of these cameras was streamed to the news organizations.

These images were uncanny, like scenes from an old movie come to life, all the stranger for being real.

All day the thing sat in the center of everyone's screens. The UFO did not move or release a puff of exhaust or change color. It remained silent, floating, and devoid of any new features to comment on beyond the thing itself. The unruffled newscasters, the true heroes of that first day, were not hindered in the least by this inconvenient inactivity. If they were skilled at nothing else, they knew how to keep their guests talking when there was nothing more to say. Hour after hour, the staid voices merely thrummed in the background, a sonic wallpaper to accentuate the footage cycled from the multiple camera angles.

Most news channels opted to let serious-looking and ashen astronomers hold court in their studios. The newscasters let them talk uninterrupted for long stretches, and talk they did. They told stories about detecting radio signals from pulsars and Fast Radio Bursts. They talked about technosignatures, Dyson Spheres, black holes, dark matter, the number of stars in the Milky Way, methane traces in the clouds of Venus, the ice-encrusted oceans of Europa, the great lakes of Titan, the Mars rovers, the Mars rock, and the Face on Mars. They talked a lot about relativity and recounted every quirky detail of Einstein's biography that they habitually trotted out for cocktail parties.

At least once every five to ten minutes, like the host of a pledge drive filling his quota of public service announcements, they pulled out of this blather to remind all the viewers that what they were looking at on their screens was even now—hard as it may be to believe—very likely not what everyone thought it was. They were oh so apologetic about spoiling the fun, but UFOs were simply not possible. Besides, if a real UFO actually did land on the White House lawn, it would not just sit there doing nothing. It would not expend the incomprehensible amounts of energy needed to come all this way just to get its picture taken like a tourist. It would send out its ambassador.

And then, on September 5th, thirty-one hours after it landed, the UFO released a bright beam of red light from its ventral side. It lanced at the White House, stopping in midair just inside of the driveway that curved beneath the South Portico. As it was registering with viewers that this was in defiance of all known physics of how light beams were supposed to work, the tip of the light began to bubble. It formed an expanding sphere the same glowing color as the beam. The sphere then elongated into an egg shape. This egg rotated and opened. Out stepped what looked like a metal man. The light beam retracted back into the craft.

The helicopter moved dead slow overhead to get a better angle for its cameras.

The visitor was not large, just over five feet tall and in the same proportions as a human body. It had two legs, two arms with hands, and a square torso, the same featureless dull gray as the skin of the UFO. An ovoid head sat atop a thick tubular neck. The face was a convex shield of what looked like polished black glass. There were no apparent joints. It took several steps toward the South Entrance door, and then planted itself in the grass at the top of the lawn.

The newscasters brought silence to their studios so that everyone could absorb what they were seeing. After an interval of several minutes, during which they judged the next remarkable development was not imminent, they began to slowly recount what had just happened, pausing within each sentence to search for the right word to characterize the red light, the egg, and the body of the visitor. And then they turned to their guests for comment. *You were saying, Mr. Astronomer.*

Only a few of them were good natured enough to fall back in their chairs and throw up their hands. The rest were wracked by a crisis of faith in their skepticism that was commensurate with their obstinacy. Some got embarrassed and angry. They yanked off their mic and stormed out of the set like this had all been an elaborate prank arranged just for them. A surprising number of them could do nothing but giggle. It was the kind of laugh that serious people involuntarily make whenever they are compelled to speak on the subject of UFOs, but now they could not stop and had to gulp water or have their mics muted. Others were unphased and undeterred, except for a slight deepening of their smirk. Occam's Razor still applied even at this late stage, they declared. An astrophysicist, the most titled national scientist on the air that day, huffed, "I'd sooner believe this is a multi-million-dollar ad campaign to get us all to go see the next Hollywood blockbuster than *that* is an alien." A very few pitched forward in awestruck wonder, studying the images with the methodical discipline of their craft, blinking furiously to whisk away the mist gathering in their eyes. They politely asked the newscaster to give them a moment.

No matter how they responded, all of them were thinking, *there goes my budget*. And they began to formulate the pitch to their funders, how the lifeless rocks and bits of photons they were studying millions or billions of miles away was in fact quite germane to this thing that was floating in the middle of Washington D.C..

To the viewers at home, the metal figure was exactly what it looked like and its appearance was the least surprising thing that could have happened. They leaned closer to their TVs. The show had begun.

BEGIN TRANSCRIPT

POTUS: Proposition. What was a national security crisis is now a diplomatic crisis with significant national security implications. We have to respond. Each of you go.

SECDEF: I agree, sir, this situation has taken on a diplomatic nature. But... I'm having a hard time picturing a proportional diplomatic response.

POTUS: They're literally knocking on our front door. We send some-one out to answer it.

CJC: We don't know enough about it. We need more data.

POTUS: The time for research was twenty years ago, or whenever it was you got wise to these things, Chairman. They're standing on my doorstep.

DNI: There has been no radio transmission, nothing from the craft. We could send the first message.

POTUS: Maybe, sure. But if they wanted to talk on the phone they would have called us, not sent out the Tinman.

DHS: There's also the technical challenge of crafting a message. How could we be sure they would understand it, not misinterpret it?

POTUS: All the more reason to send out a person. Let them take the next move after that. Feel them out. They've made their gesture. We have to make ours.

CIA: I agree with your instincts here, Mr. President. Our number one priority must be to get them to vacate our airspace immediately--

POTUS: Agreed.

CIA: The fastest way to achieve that goal is a face-to-face interaction.

POTUS: We also have to consider the public. They expect us to act. What are they going to think if we do nothing, keep hiding in our bunkers?

CIA: The public reaction, their interpretation of events, becomes more unpredictable every minute the craft sits out in the open.

POTUS: Ok, downsides to sending someone out?

SECDEF: They'll be killed. Disintegrated on live television.

CJC: Or abducted.

POTUS: Sure. But if that's what they are here for, they're going to do it. This thing lighted down in the middle of our security perimeter like a butterfly. I've read the reports on the observed capabilities of these things--reports, by the way, not one of you deemed significant enough to put on my desk until yesterday, which, you may have noticed, is too goddamn late. They're going to do what they came here to do. I'm not afraid. You all sound afraid, and you better check that quick. We will not respond from fear. We're sending someone out. The only question is who.

SECDEF: Who is our highest ranking, most expendable person?

POTUS: I hope that is a rhetorical question.

[laughter]

DNI: Would she agree to do it?

POTUS: She agrees to everything.

CIA: Can we trust that she will be... reliable?

POTUS: White always reads what we give her, and she sells it. Every time.

CIA: I mean psychologically?

POTUS: How the fuck should I know. I'm not her shrink. Anyone could crack, given the circumstances.

CIA: Not my people.

POTUS: We're not sending out G-Men to talk to the alien robot. Jesus, Harriet. Back off. ... The other factor on the table is the vote on my reform bill, which I know none of you give two shits about. But I do. This congressional cookout was posturing. The vote in the Senate was always going to be fifty-fifty. I'm going to need White to cast the tie-breaker.

SECDEF: You will need a vice president, sir. Not necessarily White.

POTUS: Yeah... Ok, thanks everyone.

ALL: Thank you, Mr. President.

POTUS: Harriet, you're taking the lead on this. I want you in the building with her.

CIA: Yes, sir. We're already in position.

POTUS: [off screen] Get Golden Boy on the phone.

END TRANSCRIPT

Susan slipped out of her pumps and paced along the glass wall of her makeshift office as she waited for the President to be patched through to the TV. The conference room windows had sweeping views of the Potomac River, the forested lip of the valley ridge, and the patchwork quilt of farmland that spread to the horizon. It was another day of pure blue, cloudless skies. Susan's gaze kept falling up into it. Events of the last day and a half had returned the sky to its antediluvian proportions. Maybe in all human history it had never been quite so immense as it seemed now, considering what had slipped out of it as if from nowhere, and what might still be up there lurking inside all that blue.

She was told to be alone for the call, which was not hard. The only people here were her family and the Secret Service agents who came in the helicopter. They were all staying in the main building of a federal research center, where the staff was accustomed to being flushed out whenever some crisis precipitated the need for a government official to be squirreled into an undisclosed location.

After lunch Brian had taken the kids to Antietam National Battlefield, which was a few miles down a country road. The visitor's center was closed but they could walk the grounds and read the inscriptions on the monuments. She could not go of course. Her campaign team had been unable to reach her, but she did not need them to tell her that visiting the site of the deadliest day in American history on the day after aliens landed would not play well.

She did look forward to joining them for ice cream later. A rumor was circulating around the compound—likely started by Chase—that an ice cream parlor in Sharpsburg was open for business. From the pictures online—wood shelves on every wall and granite countertops—the shop looked like it had been making ice cream for a hundred years, and had been a dry goods store in the century before that. It was just off of the town's one main street, which was a shallow canyon of tiny houses, aluminum frame screen doors and creaking porch swings, flower beds and narrow backyards bristling with clothes lines.

The outing would not be a photo-op where she had to try to get caught on the news projecting normalcy. There was no press or cameras for miles. The plan was to just be normal with her family for a few minutes, a little gulp of rarified air before diving down into the murky stillwater of their buffered lives. Susan did her best to arrange these moments for the four of them, especially when there was a crisis. They would take two cars. In and out before many of the town's 756 residents even noticed.

She had so far resisted the urge to look up how those 756 people voted in the last election, but she knew she would give in before leaving the compound.

When the screen blinked on, the President was already yelling. Susan was grateful it was not at her.

"The Russians? ... You all keep forgetting that I remember the Cold War. I was there. The Russians were not even close to putting a man on the Moon in 1969. The Russians could not put a man on the Moon today. The fucking Russians? And stop asking for more money for hypersonics. You're not getting another nickel for that bill of goods."

He slammed the phone into the cradle.

"Sorry, Susan. Secretary of the Air Force. I'm firing everyone, all of them. If I could have every member of my national security team stand in front of the South Portico and commit seppuku I would. We're going to clean this up so fast it will make your head spin."

"My head is already spinning, sir."

She slid into the chair at the far end of the conference table. On the monitor, mounted to the opposite wall, the President was sitting at the end of his own long table.

He squinted into his camera. "Can you... can you move closer? I feel like I'm watching a Stanley Kubrick movie."

She walked the length of the table where she vacillated between sitting in one or the other corner chairs. She decided to lean against the end of the table, directly in front of the TV. This made her face awkwardly large on the President's screen, but he thought it impolite to ask her to move again. He got to his point.

"Susan, I need you to go back to the White House. I've chosen you to deliver our welcome message in person. I'm asking. You can say no, of course, but I need your answer now."

"Of course. I will."

Susan heard these words slip out of her mouth as if she was still sitting at the far end of the room and someone else had said them. She was fully accustomed to going along with other people's plans. Hitting her marks and not dwelling on what came after, this was too often her only sense of accomplishment. Still, to agree to such a thing without making a decision at all sparked the briefest flash of doubt.

The President's hard stare drifted to the right and turned wistful. "You know, I would not mind going myself. They'd never let me. On a normal day my doctors think my ticker is about to crap out any minute. You should see the way they look at me every time I go to the bathroom. The Speaker did half-assed volunteer himself in his mealy-mouthed way. But he's older than me." Then the President gave his canned phrase that seemed to involuntarily burble out of him in every conversation she'd had with him since they first met eight years ago. "Enjoy your youth, kid."

Susan had forgotten about the fish until that moment. The ancient, mud-encrusted eye that had been watching her from her mantel for most of the years of her vice presidency, now popped into her mind's eye, slowly blinking some kind of signal. At no point since the helicopter landed had she thought at all about the conversation with Brian on the patio. Now she became vaguely aware that she had been in that moment close to some kind of revelation.

"Now I don't want you to worry," the President cooed. "We're making the exchange brief and very safe. Remember, I'm going to need you in one piece for the Senate vote."

Susan cocked an eyebrow. "That's still on? We're getting back to business that quickly?"

He leaned forward, placing his hands together on the tabletop.

"You're going to be shocked how fast everything snaps back. For a week and a day it will be the end of the world. People have to get back to their lives. They are not going to change their conception of their place in the universe based on this one event."

It was when he said things in this way that Susan was reminded of how much she loved the President. Her fondness for him was akin to what she had felt for a few professors she'd been lucky to study under in college. He was rigorous, quick with a story, patient up to a point, and almost always right. Once in a great while he left her with a nagging sense that, because of his age and body of experience, there might be some insight he was missing that was just for her to uncover, though it was rarer still when she could actually figure out what that might be. That her fondness for him was in no way reciprocated was part of the charm. This professor did not have any favorite pupils, and if he did it certainly was not her.

"When do I leave?" she asked.

"Right now. The agents are ready with the helicopter."

"Ice cream will have to wait."

He ignored this statement, and leaned into his *one more thing* stance.

"I know we agreed not to discuss the campaign. Your campaign." He waited.

"Yes, sir?"

"There is always a point in a campaign where you realize this is not going to work, or it will work. The first realization is the common one. My staff's running a betting pool where nearly all of them have picked a date in January for when you will have to withdraw. Some bet you'll do it in December to save face. No one thinks you'll make it to Super Tuesday. Not a single person."

Susan's heart sank. She did not allow herself to have these thoughts, and no one in her circle talked like this. "We're just getting started," she countered meekly.

"The country has known you for eight years. A Black woman with your background. It is just too easy to whip up both sides to hate you. We haven't seen unfavorables like yours since the election that shall not be mentioned. Golden Boy is going to skunk you."

Susan turned her face from the screen. Some high, wispy clouds were moving across the sky. She wanted nothing more than to run out of the room, find that ice cream parlor and order ten ice cream sundaes.

"But..." The President smiled. "What you are about to do, this UFO situation, will wipe all of that away."

Susan returned her attention to the screen.

"Talk about a lucky break. You have an opportunity here that no politician ever gets. The chance to demonstrate physical and moral courage. The rest of us can only tell stories. We pantomime courage. But you, Susan, get to do it live on TV."

"You really think that is how it will come off?"

"Forget Reagan squaring up against Gorbachev. This is an entirely different league. Literally everyone watching, from the rubes to the eggheads, are going to half expect they are about to watch their Vice President be vaporized by a ray gun. And yet, out you go. It is not possible to orchestrate a campaign event this compelling. After tomorrow, no one will be able to lay a finger on you. It will be like you are a different person. A new Susan White."

Susan's entire body uncoiled. Her arms and backside wilted against the edge of the table. She exhaled all the breath and tension that had been locked above her diaphragm. "That is exactly what I have been thinking about," she gushed.

Her vision of the fish, the dark thoughts about her children, the urges to quit—maybe it was all just anxiety about the state of her campaign, its impending humiliation. What she had needed all along was a different angle, a better script to follow. Now she had one. The soundbites and debate zingers started to pop in her head.

When my country called on me to handle the UFO crisis, there was no playbook to follow...

Governor, while you were watching the event on TV with everyone else, I was there...

If the President of Iran thinks he can intimidate me, I'm going to sit him down and tell him about the time I went head to head against a fricken alien robot...

A woozy smile spread across her lips. She would not even need a script writer. And the memes, of course, were going to be killer.

The President saw that Susan's mood had shifted. He leaned back in his chair, satisfied that he had sold it. Harriet Howell, his CIA Director, had coached him to say this part. The idea was to give Susan a physiological hold on normalcy—a normal campaign event with stakes she could relate to—that would keep her mind from buckling when she stared into the blank face of the Tinman. It helped that he believed it to be true. Assuming she was not actually vaporized by a ray gun, and if she succeeded in instigating the other part of Harriet's plan, the election would be Susan's to walk away with.

He stood up, placed one hand over his heart and gave a sharp nod that mimicked the solemn decorum of a salute. They would not speak again until after the job was done. He wished her luck. The screen blinked off.

Susan did a little dance where she twirled around and pounded her stockinged feet up and down on the carpet. And then the agents came in to take her away.

***

All the news networks were continuing their uninterrupted coverage. The newscasters were napping in shifts, and when they were on air sipped high octane energy drinks from their studio mugs. Network presidents were taking panicky phone calls from the makers of mattresses, gutter cleaners, and geriatric pharmaceuticals wanting to know when the commercial breaks would resume. The more incredulous scientists had run out of things to talk about. Most of them threw in the towel, or were asked by producers to go home until they could think of more things to say. Those same producers were getting an education in just how many ufologists there were in the world, in sheer amount, type, and dress code. Like the scientists, they were good talkers, and had their own scale from credulous to incredulous, albeit much further down the spectrum of extraordinary beliefs than any of the scientists dared to tread. There were those who espoused that the hard evidence pointed to visitations going back a hundred years, while others believed this had been going on long enough for the aliens to have taught algebra to the Sumerians. Once a ufologist was booked and miced in the chair, the newscaster's first question was how to pronounce the word. Was it U-F-ologist, U-F-O-logist, or Uf-ologist? Opinions varied about that too.

But by late in the day on September 5th, many millions had already turned off their televisions and set out to see the thing for themselves. Anyone with the urge to not just passively receive this event but to experience it, and who could walk or roll toward D.C., stuffed sleeping bags, clean socks, flashlights, radios into whatever backpacks or suitcases they had. Cars filled with entire families, parents with young children, college students, grandparents, neighbors, even strangers hitchhiking from the side of the road, all trickled onto the highways coming out of every state. Caravans formed in Canada, Mexico and South America, undeterred by official statements, repeated by the newscasters, that borders would not be opened under any circumstances.

The National Guard, supported by the Army, had locked down the city. Every road big and small in Maryland and Virginia within a seven-mile radius from the White House was blocked by large, beige military trucks. A second perimeter of 1.2 miles ran along the Potomac River to the west, 6th Street and U Street to the east and north, and the National Mall, which was filling up with tens of thousands of Marines and Army troops who flowed like streams of ants out of the constantly arriving Stallion and Chinook helicopters. The inner perimeter was between 15th and 17th Avenues, the Ellipse, and Lafayette Square.

Nearly a million people who lived in non-federal D.C., and the ring of towns between Bethesda, McLean, Falls Church, Annandale, and Alexandria, simply walked out their front doors. Others drove until they hit the roadblocks and walked from there. The parades of strolling civilians had no trouble sidestepping, squeezing between, and even crawling under the military vehicles blocking the roads as outnumbered and dazed soldiers and guardsmen looked on.

The one-mile perimeter had more soldiers but insufficient barricades. Army planners never thought they would need crowd control this deep into the city, and by the time they saw the first wave coming it was too late. The people, smiling politely, waving and thanking them for their service, simply walked through the cordon while all the radios velcroed to the camouflage vests squawked confusion and contradicting orders.

The leading edge of this crowd spilled across the Ellipse and walked right up to the iron fence. It was too high to scale easily, but no one was especially eager to try. The gray disc floated on the other side, close enough that someone with a strong arm could ping it with a rock. No one wanted to do that either. A collective consciousness began to thread together everyone in sight of the craft. The single mind, vibrating with contentment and awe, wordlessly agreed to give whatever it was space to do whatever it had come here to do. This was close enough.

All the while the Tinman never turned to glimpse the sea of humanity forming behind its back. It remained motionless, facing the small arched doorway at the center of the white mansion.

Susan overheard her Secret Service detail talking about a crowd that was gathering, but she had no idea of the size of it since she was brought into the White House through the tunnel system. The hand-off happened at a small blastlock that opened into the sub-basement. Here a concrete corridor and adjacent rooms appeared to be a staging area for equipment, which was still being carted in through the tunnel. Some of it looked like scanners and communications devices. The guns and heavy artillery were easier to recognize, and these were stacked to the ceiling.

Dozens of people, silent as drones, squeezed between one another and the stacks, either scanning barcodes and unpacking crates, or pushing the contents toward the service elevator. They fell into three categories. The majority wore black Kevlar armor, and their limbs bristled with guns, knives, and mysterious little black boxes. Others were covered head to foot in white radiation suits. Men and women wearing trim dark suits and ear pieces moved slower, more watchful, and with less purpose than the other two groups. There were no military uniforms in sight, which led Susan to believe that there was no one in the building who was not CIA.

While waiting for her escort, Susan thought how unreal this all felt, like she was inside of a movie. She had certainly only ever experienced anything close to the scene before her while watching some movie. As soon as this idea entered her mind, it was like a lens descended over her perception, and deep in her inner ear, her orientation of when and where she was began to spin. This was not the sub-basement of the White House. This was a film studio, a passageway that ran behind the soundstages. There was not one movie being filmed, but three. One was about commandos. The second was about mad scientists. The third was about government spies. These people were all actors coming and going from wardrobe trailers, picking up the props for their scenes. This vision seemed a more plausible interpretation of reality than what was actually happening.

One of the men in Kevlar detached from the palate of background extras, walking down the corridor directly for Susan. He introduced himself as Agent Dowdrick, and then nodded at the Vice President's Secret Service detail, who took that as a signal to turn and jog back through the tunnel.

"Good afternoon, Ma'am," Dowdrick said through a thin smile. "I am to bring you to the CIA Director."

The moment she crossed through the blastlock her brain's perception that this was all a movie intensified. She was in the movie now. This moment was like one of those long shots centered on the hero slow-walking toward whatever job had to be done. Susan felt the same loneliness and isolation that those directors painted onto their heroes' faces. Dowdrick was not going to have any more lines. She thought it would be nice if this was the kind of movie where she had a sidekick.

So it did not strike her as out of sorts when she heard a man shouting for her, his voice muffled behind one of the metal doors at the end of the corridor.

Dowdrick kept walking, but the voice kept shouting "Madam Vice President," and then, "For God's sake, get me out of here."

Bob Xenakis squeezed his face into the narrow rectangular window in the door. Susan looked to Dowdrick for permission, but he only stared at her. She turned the knob.

The room was a small office lined with leaning towers of file boxes. There was a desk. Two agents, the kind wearing suit and tie, sat on one side.

Bobby's eyes were red and puffy, like he had not slept. His normally clean-shaven face and neck was covered in gray-splotched stubble.

"How did you get in here?" Susan asked him.

"Ha. I never left."

"You ignored the evacuation order? Bobby, that's a big no-no."

Dowdrick chimed in, "It's illegal."

Bobby's lips snarled. "Whatever. You spooks don't scare me." Then his eyes bulged at Susan. "Is it still here? Is it over? Is everyone coming back?"

"It's just me. I'm meeting with Howell."

Bobby whispered in her ear. "Don't trust her. You've got to bring me with you."

Susan wanted the backup, but she was leary of testing her uncertain authority against this new pack of handlers. So instead of asking Dowdrick or stating her intention, she hooked arms with Bobby and pulled him down the corridor, laughing as she said, "You look a mess, sir. You don't keep a fresh suit in your office?"

"It's at the cleaners."

Dowdrick resumed his silent escort. The trio turned left at the service elevator and entered a stairwell. As they walked side by side Bobby explained to Susan that he had been pulling an all-nighter to prepare for the reform bill vote, and was asleep on his couch when the alarm rang. When he realized why they were being evacuated, he jumped into a closet and hid until the building was silent. The CIA arrived the next day. They found him in the Lincoln Bedroom.

That last detail shocked Susan more than anything else. "You snuck into the Residence? I've never been in the Residence."

"The right window has the best view." Bobby's eyes puddled and his voice quivered. "I watched him come out. He was right there... If the window opened, I could have said hello.... He doesn't have a face. It's all black. But there's a glow coming out of it. And I swear I saw something inside of it that does not look mechanical."

They entered a tier of the underground complex that Bobby and Susan were more familiar with. It was a wider corridor with walls of heavy stone, carpeting, lit by polished lamps.

Bobby leaned in her ear again. "Ma'am, Susan, this is the moment some of us have been dreaming about. Our entire society is going to be turned upside down. Forget the politics. Human culture is going to change. Human nature is going to change. But—" he pointed at Dowdrick's back "—they're going to try to make it like it never happened."

This was the same kind of paranoid and cynical assessment she was used to hearing from Bobby. Expecting the worst out of people was always a beneficial mindset for a White House chief of staff. In this case though Susan worried that he was not thinking clearly.

"The cat's out of the bag," she said. "How can they?"

"I don't know, but they're going to try. They've kept their heads in the sand for eighty years. They don't know any other way."

Dowdrick led them to another stairwell, one that climbed into the main building.

Susan stopped him. "The Situation Room is this way."

Dodwrick turned on the first step. "The Director is in the Oval."

Bobby laughed. "Of course she is. The maniac. I bet she's sitting in his chair. Christ."

Harriet Howell was not sitting in the President's chair. She sat in the small square chair pressed to the left side of the desk with the phone tight to her ear. One pearl earring sat on the desktop. Her thin, small frame—she was not five feet tall—was poised on the edge of the seat. Her back was elegantly arched with her characteristic perfect posture, and her legs were angled sharply at the knees so that her heels, just barely able to reach the floor, could grab against the leg of the chair.

When she noticed Susan standing in the transom left of the fireplace, her eyes narrowed on the short, stocky man who appeared to be hiding behind the Vice President. She waved them both in nonetheless and motioned for them to take the two chairs facing the desk.

The West Wing offices were untouched since the evacuation and mostly deserted. There was no sign of any of the equipment from the tunnel. Four of the Director's lieutenants sat on the two couches in the center of the Oval Office, each studying computer screens opened on their laps. As soon as Susan and Bobby came in, they exited through the other door.

Harriet was in her late sixties, which made her one of the younger chiefs of the administration. When the President picked her to lead the CIA she was not well known in town, having spent much of her career overseas working in distant outposts and black sites in the dusty, ungovernable regions of the world. Not even the most connected national security reporters could confirm when or how she started in the agency. One detail of her biography they could confirm was that she had been classically trained as a ballerina since she was a girl. The rumor that never made it into print was that in the last decade of the Cold War she was a spy who used traveling Eastern European dance troupes as cover.

To Susan the Director looked no different tonight than she did in any of the meetings they had been in together over the years. Thin, curly wisps of reddish blond hair arrayed around her face, which was adorned with the pearl earrings and no makeup. She wore a cream silk blouse with a ruffled necktie that piled high around her throat, an emerald green jacket with wide lapels, and a black knee-length skirt. Harriet dressed the same as she did in the Seventies, from a wardrobe she had inherited from her mother who died from cancer when she was in college.

Bobby, who thought twice about entering the room at all, circled the chair where she had directed him to sit, before finally planting himself behind it and gripping its back with both hands like it was a shield. He and Harriet had long shared an unspoken understanding. She knew that he was interested in UFOs, and that for years he had been pushing this President and previous ones to disclose government-held secrets about them. He suspected that whatever the shape of the government's black project on UFOs, however deep its tendrils penetrated into other agencies and departments, Harriet was the one cabinet member who at least knew of its existence. He also knew that she would not allow any degree of disclosure under any circumstances, up to and including the circumstances they found themselves in tonight.

"I beg your pardon," Harriet apologized after hanging up the phone. "That was the President. He just signed off on the final language."

She swept across the office with the rigid bearings and stern gaze of a dance instructor casing her studio.

"I want to personally thank you, Madam Vice President. You were the first person we asked, but if you had said no I don't think we could have found anyone else."

"I'm happy to do it," Susan demurred.

Harriet's mouth muscles approximated the technical dimensions of a smile. There was no warmth in it. "How do you feel?"

"I'm ready."

"Good. Sit."

The Director did a quick scan of the room, looking in every direction but where Bobby stood. She ignored him completely. Her eyelids were often as they were now, drawn down and gripping the edges of her eyes like she was focusing on something in dim light. When she was satisfied with the layout, she looked to Dowdrick who was still standing in the transom. "Go to the South Entrance. The Vice President will meet you there in ten minutes." He turned and was gone, and the three of them were alone, settling into their chairs.

"Ten minutes?" Susan had lost track of time since entering the tunnel, but she could tell from the patch of sky visible through the colonnade and Rose Garden shrubbery that it was well after nightfall. "Are we going to have enough light for the cameras?"

Harriet gave an assuring nod. "The entire South Lawn is floodlit. You're going to look great, cinematic even. The truth of the matter is we do not have a minute to spare. We have to do this now." She slid a set of glossy photographs off the desk and handed them to Susan.

Sussan and Bobby hunched together and squinted into them. They looked more like pointillist paintings than satellite images. Every street, lot, and park abutting the White House fence was packed with people. The Ellipse, sections of the Mall that were not being used as a landing ground, the Capitol steps, the Lincoln Memorial, even Arlington Cemetery was carpeted with human beings.

"These were taken just before sunset. We estimate there are ten million people out there, growing by the hour. The longer the craft and the Tinman are present, the more unpredictable and volatile the crowd's behavior will become."

Susan shot Bobby a look that cautioned him not to react. He extended his chin, pressed his lips as far down his face as they could go, and jiggled his head.

Next Harriet handed Susan a printout of her script. It was three sentences, every word of it boilerplate stuff that Susan had delivered to countless visiting dignitaries, except for the last sentence.

"Paracelsius C?"

"Paracelsus C," Harriet corrected.

Susan tried again. "The crater Paracelsus C."

She handed the page to Bobby who read it glancingly, his chin and lips descended even further, before handing it back.

"Will they even understand me?"

"We have high confidence that they understand English. In the event that they do not, we have a contingency." Harriet's precise hands returned to the desktop and with swift and exact movements removed a rectangular metal plate from a cloth covering. She lifted it by pressing the tips of her fingers against two sides to avoid smudging the polished surface.

Susan figured by its weight that it was titanium. It was etched with a pictograph and numbers that looked like coordinates. On the left side was the outline of the eastern seaboard with a tiny fine-line grid of Washington D.C., and on the right were two large circles representing both sides of the Moon, each with a precise chart of all the seas and craters. A looping geometric line spiraled across the plate from the D.C. coordinates to the location on the Moon. A honeycomb of straight lines crisscrossed both images, with the small shape of a satellite at each angle point. These lines shimmered up and down the color spectrum as the plate shifted in her hands.

It was a complex, beautiful piece of craftsmanship. Susan imagined it behind a glass case in the Smithsonian after this was all over. That is if Harriet ever declassified its message and the story of what she was about to do with it.

"Just so I understand my job here... I'm to tell them to leave immediately and land their craft in a crater on the far side of the Moon, where we can resume the conversation through the satellite network?"

Harriet nodded.

Bobby had returned his face to its usual dimensions, but he was now slouched down in the chair, uncharacteristically quiet.

"Would you like to practice the lines with me?"

Susan read the paper again. She closed her eyes and repeated them silently to herself. When her eyes opened she said, "I've got it. I'm ready. I just need a moment to freshen up."

Harriet stood up while lifting a black briefcase that had been leaning against her chair. Susan and Bobby raised eyebrows at each other as she popped it open on the President's desk. It was full of wigs.

"We collected them from your house," Harriet explained. "I hope you don't mind."

The one thing that had been giving Susan pause was the thought of going out in front of the cameras with her hair in braids. They were tight and holding up fine, having been done less than a week ago, but they completely clashed with her suit.

Susan pulled the straightest, darkest one and a pic and stepped into the small bathroom. When the wig was placed just like she wanted it, she caught her eyes in the mirror, and the enormity of what was about to happen almost took her breath. But the moment passed just as quickly. None of what was happening around her felt real enough to penetrate. She was still giddy with thoughts of how invincibly popular she was about to become. The campaign event fiction that Harriet had implanted in her mind had not only steadied her nerves but anesthetized her imagination. The meeting would go exactly as planned. She would read her greeting, present the plate, the UFO would fly off, and then this weekend she would go on *Meet the Press* and tell the whole story.

When she came out, Harriet was standing in the door in the left bend of the Oval. She said she was going to the bunker where she would monitor the meeting, and where they would reconvene when the encounter was over. When Susan asked why she was going to the bunker, Harriet feigned candor.

"The next move is ours. It will solicit a reaction. We must be prepared for the worst. Besides, this little detail will make for a juicy leak to *The New York Times.*"

Susan took that in, and then asked why this meeting had not been held in the bunker.

"If I'm being honest," Harriet started without a trace of irony, "I just thought this may be the last time anyone ever uses this office. I wanted it to be for this. Chin up, ma'am."

She gave two final directives—stick to the script, and by no means engage in a longer conversation—and was gone.

Susan picked up the titanium plate and walked with Bobby through the offices toward the ground floor of the White House.

"You were quiet in there," she prodded, gently gouging her knuckles into Bobby's shoulder.

He grunted. "My grandmother had a saying. After the cake is baked, there is nothing to do but eat it."

The vaulted Center Hall was packed end to end with the sensor equipment and weaponry that had been brought through the tunnel. Dishes and rods and other contraptions slowly waved side to side. Agents in white suits manned banks of computer monitors. Large artillery guns and ordinance were mounted against the back wall. A phalanx of agents in black armor stood ready with their long guns pointed at the inlaid marble floor. Susan and Bobby walked between them as if invisible. The scientists never lifted their gaze from their screens and readouts. The commandos kept their eyes locked on the door to the Diplomatic Reception Room.

Susan and Bobby lingered in the heavy white-paneled transom. They both knew without saying so that this was as far as they would go together.

This large oval room, with its wrap-around mural of crowds of happy 19th Century Americans strolling through verdant landscapes, was also crammed with equipment and weapons and black-clad agents. All the high-backed armchairs and shiny wooden tables were pushed into a heap. A grandfather clock lay on its side, spilling its innards of weights and chains and smashed glass. The crystal face was cracked with the minute and hour hands dangling. George Washington was left in place to survey the defensive line from his portrait above the fireplace mantel.

At the opposite end of the room was the narrow vestibule that led to the South Entrance doors. Two large guns on tripods stood on either side, their long barrels angled into the vestibule. Dowdrick, legs spread and arms akimbo, had planted himself between the two guns and kept watch on the motionless figure of the Tinman that was visible through the glass panes of the outer doors.

The room and hall were silent except for humming hard drives and the occasional clicks of the final weapons being assembled.

"The plan makes sense, right?" Susan whispered. "There are ten million people out there, with more on the way. It's not safe."

"Not safe for the status quo. Not safe for the entire basis of their right to rule. Not safe for the arbiters of official reality. They're going to make it like this never happened."

Susan laughed. "How?"

"I don't know. They'll find a way. They'll make everyone think this was a movie they saw once. A Harriet Howell production."

The pair had been staring at the South Entrance door and Dowdrick's broad, padded back, but now searched one another's eyes. Her eyes were wide and jittery. His were grim and barely open. All of Bobby's spunky energy had leaked out of him since leaving the Oval

Office. He looked like he was about to fall asleep against the door jamb.

His next words were slow and faint. "Susan, you have to tell them to do something that will leave a mark. They can't just fly away this time. Tell them to leave a mark."

Dowdrick turned sideways and called across the room. "Madam Vice President, I'm going to open the doors. Mr. Xanakis, please step aside."

Susan's gaze flitted between the two men. She could not quite conceive of what Bobby was trying to tell her. But his demeanor now and since she found him in the basement made her think that maybe he had a better understanding of what was happening than anyone else. It was almost like he had expected all of this to happen, that he was somehow prepared for it. She thought he might be the better person to talk to the Tinman. These were vague emotions, stirred by an increased heart rate. The most dominant one was that she was about to be all alone and she did not want to be.

"You should come with me," she blurted.

Bobby, who was already stepping backward into the hall, forced a smile. "No way. I've got young kids."

Two girls, Callie and Sara. He had grown kids too, and he liked to joke that these two were a consolation prize to his third wife. He loved them enough to coach softball, and hang their pictures behind his desk, and never bring them to congressional cookouts. He left the office early most days to have dinner with them, except the day the UFO landed.

"Besides," he said, as an agent gently took his forearm, "it's not in the script."

Susan turned toward Dowdrick who had a hand on each doorknob, his arms primed to spring open the doors. Another agent, standing on the wings of the American Eagle in the carpet in the middle of the room, bobbed his hand in the air while counting down from five on his fingers.

She took a deep breath, and as she held it, turned for one last look at Bobby. The agent was behind him on the bottom steps of the Center Hall staircase. As they disappeared up the stairwell, Susan thought she saw the agent slip something around his wrists.

When she faced forward again, the doors were open. Dowdrick had pressed himself against the vestibule wall, out of the Tinman's line of sight.

It was a cue not any different from an appearance on a talk show. She straightened her suit and used her strides across the carpet to roll into her walk-on-stage stance. Out she went through the small archway, her heels clicking across the marble pavers. There was no red carpet or any other attempt at ceremony, not even a flag. Only herself.

She stopped on the edge of the landing, flanked on both sides by the curved staircases that wrapped up to the portico. Here she counted down ten seconds. This was the first part of Harriet's choreography.

The row of floodlights that had been mounted along the roof of the White House covered everything—the grass and trees, the craft and its passenger—in stark, white light. It was the same light as standing in a floodlit football field late at night. This bubble of artificial day reflected off the heavy cloud cover that had settled in over the city, which in turn illuminated the massive crowd that receded from the White House fence.

The people closest to the fence could see that a person had come out of the building. Those in the crowd with binoculars spread word that it was the Vice President. When this news ripped backward through the dense core of hundreds of thousands, a euphoric, roaring cheer rolled with it. And they were a mere tip of the mallet knocking against the millions beyond them like a bell. Their toll shook the entire city.

Susan liked the sound of that. She had never gotten crowds like this. No one in history had. But she kept her eyes on her mark.

As unusual as these circumstances were, the experience was in no way unsettling for Susan. From across the driveway the Tinman did not look alien at all. It had the size and proportions of an average human with no remarkable markings or features on its surface. She had seen stranger robots working the front desk of Japanese hotels. Even the black, faceless front of the head seemed familiar, like a blank iPhone screen. She wondered if the conversation she was about to have would be like talking to Siri.

And so she moved toward it with the same perky stride she would use if she was approaching a governor or celebrity waiting on a tarmac or rally stage.

The Tinman's boxy feet were planted in the lawn about six feet from the driveway. Susan planted her black Jimmy Choo block-heel pumps on the edge of the pavement. Her stage smile lifted out of habit, and then froze part way up her face as she became aware of the fact that she was in the presence of something truly alien. The metal—if it was metal—emitted a wispy, marbled sheen. The translucent texture made it seem like she could put her hand through it, no more solid than a thick fog. There were no joints or seams or even crease marks, implying that when it moved it did so more like a fluid. The black face appeared solid, like glass, but it was not blank. Inky black tendrils undulated within the black orb.

Susan stared into these unearthly things, feeling herself become hypnotized by them. Her consciousness was freefalling into a dark pool, snuffing out her bodily senses one by one. First to go was her sense of the passage of time, which she had been minding. Harriet's script was measured in seconds. The entire encounter was to last no longer than two minutes, and only that if the pleasantries ran long. No different than media appearances where she had intervals of thirty to forty seconds to land her talking points, for which much practice had wired a timer into her subconscious that ticked away without her having to think about it. Now she found herself unsure how long she had been standing there staring into the black face. Time itself, even the air all around her, was congealing into a viscous fluid in which she was floating, immobile.

A little head shake helped to regain her focus. She closed and opened her eyes, then completed her smile, and tried to remember her lines.

Before she could say them, the row of searing lights above her blinked out. So did every light across the city. She and the Tinman and everything else were plunged into darkness.

Then she heard the voice.

Susan. Hello.

Her pupils adjusted. The murky liquid within the Tinman's head was dimly lit by a purplish light shining up from within the chest cavity. The fleshy tendrils moved as though connected to multiple, separate unseen nodes. Each had a lateral ridge specked with bluish-white beads of light that were slowly becoming brighter.

The voice repeated its greeting.

Hello. Susan.

It was a human voice, neither male nor female nor electronic. She did not hear it in the normal way, as sound waves coming out of the Tinman's voicebox. In fact she could hear no sound at all, not the roaring crowd, and not the thwacking helicopter, which seemed to not be there anymore. It was like her ears had been taken offline.

The Tinman's voice was coming from inside of her brain. She could literally feel resonances gently rippling through the folds of her gray matter. The vibrations were situated in the front of her head above her eyes, the part of the brain that processes language. She could not remember from science class what it was called. The voice enunciated its words crisply but with a gentle, caressing affect. They were silky and soft, and they swayed like the tendrils swayed. It made her feel calm and at peace.

Without thinking of how or why, Susan responded to the voice with her thoughts. She had to concentrate. It was like putting each word in a bubble and blowing them one by one toward the tendrils.

I. am. Susan.

Hello Susan

Hello.

We are here for you. We would like you to come with us.

Where. ?

We would like you to come with us to a place that your star charts call PZ Cassiopeiae.

Cass. Io. Peia. ?

Yes.

Why. ?

Because you are needed there.

For. What. ?

The voice fell quiet for what seemed like a long time. Susan still had no sense of time. It was long enough for her to long for the voice to come back.

I am sorry Susan. The answer to your question cannot be understood in this medium.

That's convenient.

Susan's engrained cynicism shoved that complete thought into the bubble all by itself. It made the process come easier. Her voice-thoughts now became looser, more at ease.

After another long pause, the voice returned.

A desire to understand motivation is a sensible one for those with a biological and ecological fixation on abundance and scarcity. It is not the only basis for trust.

You sound like my therapist.

And like her therapist, the voice did not respond to her deflectionary quips. It waited.

Why me?

Because you came through the door.

Susan moved her gaze away from the Tinman for the first time. At the bottom of the lawn, she saw dark figures wedged between the bars and inching their way to the top of the fence. Her body swirled around through the thickness. A silhouette shaped like Dowdrick stood within the archway with more silhouettes lining up behind him.

She asked the voice, *Can I come back?*

Yes. But it will be a long time from now. People here will be in a different stage of their evolution.

In a good way or a bad way?

That will be up to them to choose. You may say no, Susan. But you must decide quickly. The men with the guns will come for you soon.

I want to go with you.

The voice changed slightly. The impression it made on her brain was full of sadness. Or maybe, Susan thought, it was reflecting her own descent into sorrow.

Your husband Brian. Your children, Emma and Chase. You will never see them again.

I understand.

The journey will be long. You will be... Another long pause... *uncomfortable for much of it. When we reach our destination, you will become a different person.*

The voice felt Susan trying hard to remember something. It withdrew from her thoughts.

She knelt in the grass, trying to ground herself by running her fingers through the stiff blades. With closed eyes she tried to summon the images of her children's faces. Chase's pudgy cheeks and round nose like her own. Emma's pointy nose, like Brian's. It was surprisingly tricky. The whole image was a pixelated blur except for the feature where she put her focus, and some features—the hairline, the ears, the chin—were gray blotches. Before she could complete the full face, her memory swiped to the next image.

The last image in the scroll was of Chase and Emma's faces contorting from bleary eyed sleep to fear as they were shoved onto the helicopter. If the President had taken another hour to make his decision, she would have gotten to see her kids today. They would have met up at the ice cream parlor in Sharpsburg. If everyone was in a good enough mood, they might have shared some laughs. Brian would almost certainly have been a gibbering nervous wreck. Chase was quick with dark, dry jokes that always landed perfectly in those moments. *Good thing you lost that primary, mom, or it would have been your house blown up like Independence Day.* Emma would sullenly pick at her ice cream—whatever flavor was purple, like she always ordered ever since she was a baby—until she tired of Chase's jokes. Then, in her stentorian debate team voice, she would launch into whatever thesis she had been mulling. *The Psycho-Social Threat to a Constitutional Order Posed by a UFO Landing on the White House Lawn.* Then Chase would think of more jokes. Susan, like most nights at the dinner table, would moderate the ensuing squabble while also keeping it going with prods and open-ended questions. She loved watching them go at it, each sibling refusing to give an inch to the other's brilliance.

There they were. She had their faces fully formed now.

If Susan had one wish it would be that she could have had that last moment with them, and the memory of it to take with her. She was long used to feeling guilty about lost time, but the sorrowful gratitude welling in her heart had no trace of guilt. Missing out on the ice cream parlor was not the same as missing a birthday because her boss told her to be somewhere at the last minute. She chose this on her own. At every step of that choice—when she said yes, when she got into the helicopter without saying goodbye, when she entered the tunnels, when she walked away from Bobby and out the door—some deep-sleeping part of herself understood how this was going to end. She had known deep down that once she faced the Tinman, no matter the details of its message, there could be no going back to how things were. The President and his CIA Director thought they were tricking her into doing this. The truth was that Susan had tricked herself. The part of her that wanted this—the layer of crusted, fossilized consciousness deep within, the remnant of every extinct species whose DNA was intertwined with hers—somehow gave her enough cover to take the leap out of her life and into another one.

That consciousness was in charge now.

Susan opened her eyes and lifted her hand from the grass to the phone in her coat pocket. The photo app had thousands of pictures of her family. She had snapped most of them seconds after prodding and begging for her kids to stand up straight and smile—*not that way, the right way*—with square after square of the exact same pose. It was comforting to know that at any point on her journey through the lightyears and centuries she could reach for the phone and scroll through those memories. But it did not seem right or necessary that Emma and Chase—and even photogenic Brian who always smiled best the first time—should be permanently memorialized across the universe by digital bits that would not only outlast the real people on a cosmic time scale but would also eventually override Susan's own true memories of them.

She set the black slab on pavement beside the titanium plate that was lying face down, which she did not recall having dropped. As she stood up, she noticed Dowdrick had moved outside. Rows of black-clad commandos were filing behind him, their rifles pointed at the ground.

She was about to tell the voice it had better hurry with whatever it was going to do, but a new kind of doubt seized her. She had always gone along to get along with other people's plans, and she wondered if this was no different.

Before we go, Susan said to the voice, *I'm going to need you to try a little harder to explain why this is happening.*

The voice, though not impatient, rolled a tick faster into her consciousness.

We have been making our presence known to you for one of your centuries. Some of your people, like your friend Bobby, are aware of these encounters. Many, even among those who experienced them, are not. Our history has taught us that it is important to tread lightly and reveal ourselves gradually. It is the way of gods to call out of the sky with a loud voice. Since we are not gods, we are careful not to be mistaken for them. We are like any other natural phenomenon. We believe as you believe.

You seemed to have changed your strategy.

We have never encountered such stubborn people. Acceptance usually does not take this long. It is time for us to go, so we chose a final encounter that is most suited to your perception of reality. We do apologize for the crowd. It is not our preferred way.

What is your preferred way?

You are. On the craft, you will meet someone like you. When we reach PZ Cassiopeiae, you will be that someone for someone else. Are you ready, Susan?

Susan nodded.

The lawn bloomed with light. Horizontal shafts of blinding whiteness radiated out from beneath the UFO. The light enveloped the trees, the White House, and the crowd on the Ellipse as the craft shot straight up and came to a sudden stop one hundred feet in the air. The entire underside of the UFO blazed like a megawatt spotlight.

The Tinman lifted its legs and began to move back down the lawn, following the same path it had walked at noon that day. Susan walked beside it. They crossed the bottom section of the circular driveway and then passed around the fountain. As they neared the circle of fried, brown grass where the UFO had been hovering, Susan turned to the crowd. She took a few steps away from the Tinman toward the fence, lifted her right arm and waved.

The millions who saw her roared louder than before.

A year to the day from that moment, on that exact spot, the President would dedicate a larger-than-life statue of Susan frozen in bronze in that pose. The sculptor said in interviews that she spent the most time of her commission trying to get the odd angle of the waggling wrist just right.

Two bright red beams lanced out of the center of the UFO. The tips hit the ground and ballooned into large spinning eggs that swept slowly toward Susan and the Tinman. The voice told her to walk into the light.

"Wait," Susan said, using her real voice.

The voice began to pump reassuring vibes into her brain, but stopped when Susan grabbed the Tinman's arm and pulled the black glass of its face close to hers.

"Siri?"

The voice warbled through her gray matter in what Susan interpreted as a laugh.

"Siri, play Ascension by Maxwell."

The voice did not play the song, but it did assure her that there was music where they were going.

Susan stepped inside the egg and out of Earth's gravity well. The UFO drifted across the sea of upturned, weeping faces, and then, in an instant, zipped into the clouds out of sight.

***

Before the week was out, the Senate confirmed Brad Allen as the new Vice President. On the same day, he cast the tie-breaking vote on the President's entitlement reform bill. Within five fiscal years, the law exceeded CBO projections by reducing the federal budget deficit by twenty-three percent.

In the days following her disappearance on the UFO, the former Vice President's approval rating reached the highest on record. For every year after that, for the rest of human history—at least as long as scientific polling data was available—Susan White was voted most admired person.

| 2 |

Ubuntu

It was the meeting after the meeting when the Four 'Yan Fashi figured out how to end democracy in America. Three secretaries of state, each phoning in from their controlling piece of the Electoral College map, had ended the fateful conference call with a gentlemen's agreement to decline to certify the results of the presidential election, which had been lost and won five weeks earlier. The math of that election had not been in Mwizi's favor. Now it was.

Of the five swing states Mwizi lost that were also controlled by his party, only two were needed. The third secretary of state joined the group to bring political cover to the other two. He was also a political pugilist whose voters expected him to be tough on election security, and this would be a fun way to get the governorship for himself. It was his idea to put the ask to the Four 'Yan Fashi. A distraction. Nothing unseemly or illegal, just any old thing to absorb the media for a few weeks until Christmas. A national event that would drown out the primal screams in their urban cores and block the protests from spilling into the suburban ring and up the exurban corridors. They would sign what needed to be signed, and go before the cameras to say what needed to be said, but they did not want anyone thinking about it for too long.

Muongo, Ògbòó, and Sasabonsam charged into the residence with the good news. The hard part was over. By Safe Harbor Day, next

Tuesday, only forty-seven states will have submitted their certified Electoral College votes. Come January 6, all Congress had to do was count them. The vice president would announce the plain fact that Mwizi had more than his opponent.

They dropped into the armchairs around a central coffee table and began strategizing the distraction.

Mwizi, still in his bathrobe, did not move from the window. A towering snowsquall was slowly eating the parkland and granite slabs, with half of the sky clear blue. The sunshine shot through the wall of snow turning it dirty yellow. The light this cast into his living room was like illuminated smog, beautiful and foul all at once.

For the first time in four years, the tension coiled around Mwizi's soul slackened just a bit. The outcome of the conference call was not a surprise, for he knew the type of men who were on that call. Out of his five options, he had picked them because of the type of men they were. Two were the best of the cutthroats, other than himself. The other a weakling. Their ask was an interesting challenge, but he had anticipated that too. There was always an ask.

While the others discussed the secretaries' request, Mwizi shuffled between the window and the screen in the opposite corner that played his favorite daytime-TV game show. For an hour each weekday he watched the contestants solve a series of puzzles and then guess at doors that concealed prizes. Half of the prizes were vacation packages and expensive home appliances, while the other half were worthless. Mwizi's contribution to the discussion around his coffee table was interlaced with curses lobbed at the strategic folly of the contestants on his TV.

Each of the Four 'Yan Fashi had their own idea for what would make a good distraction. Ògbòó's idea was shot down first. Releasing the latest oppo research on the Democrat would not make a ripple in the tsunami of a newscycle they would be raising. Seven-year-old stolen company emails hinting at an inappropriate office relationship was a weak smear by their usual standards. The opposition media would ignore it in any case.

Sasabonsam suggested using the military. "Something easy, like invading Cuba."

This was considered for half of the duration of Mwizi's game show. It would create a rally around the flag that just might do the trick. Not everyone would buy it, but they only needed some of the people. *'It's time to support the troops'* would at least be something for the three secretaries to say while they hustled past reporters in their state capitals. Even the media got in line when the boys and girls in uniform were sent into harm's way.

But the plan did not sit well with Ògbòó, who had a son in the Navy. He also had to appease an unruly caucus of hawks and isolationists, chickenshits all. None of the three had a veto over another, but since Ògbòó was speaker of the house, the others agreed to table it unless other ideas did not pan out.

An elderly butler, whose lurching footfalls were as quiet as the snow swirling against the window panes, came in from the hall. The 'Yan Fashi did not even know he had entered until he set an ice bucket filled with cans of Diet Rite on the coffee table. Their conversation stopped until he completed his soundless circuit of the room and was out the door. A sudden burst of jeers from the game show drew their eyes to the TV.

Mwizi grabbed a can and sipped from it as he paced. Diet Rite was his preferred drink. He really did like the taste, although on his first day in the White House he had issued a directive that all food products purchased by the kitchen staff had to be off brand. Though he was exceedingly cheap, this was as much out of spite as thrift. It had been a shock to learn that he was expected to pay for his own meals. The chef quit after one week. This did not trouble Mwizi, who had a life-long habit of working through meals and eating once a day. He had no gustatory appetites. By some quirk of genetics or upbringing his pallet watered for no food. Consequently, he was too thin for his six-foot-two frame and carried himself pitched forward with a lean and hungry look.

Most of his meals now came out of little cartons of chalky green protein supplement that he drank from his desk. It was called Succulent. Sasabonsam owned the company that made it.

Long before becoming Mwizi's chief of staff, Sasabonsam went to Silicon Valley with nothing but a trust fund and some incipient survivalist and anarchist-adjacent political philosophies. Becoming a billionaire had only entrenched them.

One of his pet projects had been to form an independent nation state on a chain of reclaimed oil platforms in international waters. A nation of no laws. Their main food supply—until they learned hydroponics—was to be Succulent, which was why he bought out the company. Unfortunately the product was not as nutritious as advertised. After a storm stranded the new nation for several months without a communication system, some had to resort to cannibalism. During congressional testimony Sasabonsam assured his interrogators that it was only a few isolated cases, and only after the corpse had died of natural causes.

Boxes of the stuff were stacked in an Oval Office closet, purchased at discount of course.

Muongo spoke next. He prefaced his suggestion with the disclaimer that he was not speaking from his official capacity as CIA Director.

"What if we ask our Russian friends to stage a light cyber attack?"

The other two nodded themselves into agreement with the good idea.

"Shutdown their Instagram," chirped Ògbòó. "Delete Netflix. That'll do it."

"More serious than that," Muongo replied. "But temporary. A hydroelectric dam or nuclear plant. Everyone's scared shitless for the one week that we need."

The Four 'Yan Fashi fell quiet, and the plan seemed settled.

Then Mwizi stepped into the circle of chairs and killed it with a chop of his hand. "Do you know how many favors they'll call in for something like that? We'll all be buying dinner for every oligarch and his whores for the rest of our lives."

He returned to the window. The snow was thick now, concealing the sun, the granite, even the trees on the sloping lawn.

On the game show, the final round was building to its climax. The winning contestant picked the third door. Lucky No. 3.

"Oh I think you're going to like this," the host crooned, pulling the card from his breast pocket. The rowdy audience fell silent.

"A five-star resort. A hotel and casino with views that are—out—of—this—world…"

Mwizi considered his view into white nothingness. The world was blotted out. The entire universe compressed into a flat wall. A thought occurred to him, an almost pleasing notion, that if he could build a wall like that two feet from this window, and never leave, never have to speak to another person ever again, he would like that very much. It gave him a flicker of cheer.

"My friend," drawled the game show host, "You've just won an all-expenses-paid vacation for two…"

Mwizi looked over his shoulder just in time. Door Number Three flew up, revealing the prize.

"…to Planet X!"

The prize was a flying saucer, made of cardboard and silver spray paint. A bare-legged woman goose stepped about in a skintight, bright green leotard and an enormous paper mache, bug-eyed alien head bobbling on her shoulders.

The trombones sounded. All was lost. "Idiot," Mwizi muttered as he shut off the TV.

It was the answer he needed.

Mwizi stepped behind Sasabonsam, placing his hands on the shoulders of his suit—a trim, rust colored Brioni that cost many times more than the combined value of the other suits in the room. His withered hands massaged the fine threads, not in a friendly way.

"This guy's been trying to get me to release the UFO files since we got here. What about those?"

Sasabonsam remained stiff and mute as a mannequin for the rest of the meeting-after-the-meeting.

"It'll scare the hell out of people," Mwizi explained, "and it won't cost me a thing."

Ògbòó looked to Muongo. "We do have UFO files, right? That's, like, uh…. a real thing?"

He shrugged. "Let me check on it."

Mwizi returned to the window and the all-consuming snow. "Check whatever the fuck you want. But do it."

Door No. 1

Remarks by the President Announcing the Truth About UFOs

December 3, 2028 | Speeches & Remarks

8:01 P.M. EST

THE PRESIDENT: My Fellow Americans,

At Noon on July 8, 1947, Colonel William Blanchard issued a press release stating that the United States Army had recovered a "flying disc" from another planet. Three days earlier a local rancher had called Blanchard's base to complain that something large had crashed on his property. The Army collected the debris, which was then flown to 8th Air Force headquarters in Fort Worth, Texas, for study. Before the crash evidence had even arrived, the commander of the 8th Air Force, Brigadier General Roger Ramey, ordered a second press release.

At Three O'clock PM, July 8, the Army announced that a weather balloon had crashed in that rancher's field. The three hours between those two statements on July 8, 1947 was a turning point in the history of our country, and in the history of the entire world.

I come before you tonight to report that the first press statement was the correct one.

Colonel Blanchard was the commander of a base in south-east New Mexico that was then called Roswell Army Air Force Base. His press release was the first time the government of the United States officially acknowledged the existence of extraterrestrial life visiting the Earth. Today, eighty-one years later, is the second.

The next morning at CIA headquarters, as Muongo walked the long hall to the director's suite, his deputy spotted him through his open office door. He banged his desk and hailed "Pete" with such exuberance that Muongo startled and sloshed his coffee on the floor.

Being director for over a year had still not acclimated him to what an oddly cheerful workplace this was. Before he was the chief political advisor on Miwizi's campaign, he was a single-term congressman and an executive for a pharmaceutical company. All he knew of the CIA was from Jack Ryan movies. He could not understand why all these spies had a literal open-door policy and called everyone, including himself, by first names.

The deputy rushed into the hall waving the transcript. "Have you seen this?"

Muongo skimmed the first page. There were many others stapled to it.

"Who's writing this?"

"Who do you think? Bat boy."

For even the Four 'Yan Fashi called Sasabonsam a vampire since he resembled the creature from their comic books. Pale skin. High, hairless forehead. Sharp teeth, and eyes that were nearly all black. That, and the fact that he stalked through the offices long after everyone went home for the night, scheming ways to enact his strange political views.

Muongo handed over his coffee and leafed through the rest of the speech.

"This is really happening?" asked the deputy.

Muongo whistled. "It's on like Donkey Kong."

When they reached the director's suite, they found the doors already opened and a small gathering in the inner office. The Director of National Intelligence, the Under Secretary of Defense for Intelligence & Security, and the commander of Air Force Intelligence stood in a triangle formation, arms crossed, speaking in hushed, grim tones. His own Director of Science and Technology, from two floors down, was pacing in a wide circle around them. He seemed to be having some trouble breathing.

They were just the sort of mid-level careerists that Mwizi had put Muongo in charge of the CIA to protect him from. Since his first day on the job he had imagined the intervention happening in exactly this way. He had been preparing. The Russia House purge. The wiretapping scheme. The bloody little mishap in Guatemala. No one ever showed up until today, and they were all holding copies of Sasabonsam's speech. Muongo was dazed. *This* is what brought them? He tried to remember all the threats he had practiced.

The DNI broke away and approached him. Mwizi no longer invited him to meetings because he always banged on about the gray areas of law and where the spirit of the Constitution resides. They had let him stay on because he looked too old to get out of bed. He had gotten out of bed that morning.

"Pete," the DNI said warmly as he took Muongo's meaty hand between both of his papery ones. With a grandfatherly twinkle in his eyes he said, "We're coming to you like this because you know him."

Muongo flapped the pages of the speech in his face. "You're telling me this shit's real?"

The twinkle dimmed. "Would you mind if we close the door?"

By mid-afternoon, Muongo was in an SUV wending its way toward the White House. The Under Secretary of Defense for Intelligence & Security sat across from him, reading aloud from a thick briefing book open on his lap. There were proprietary interests to consider. For over fifty years, taxpayer money had been socked away in private aerospace through Special Access Programs, black projects that no one in Congress was ever told about. Billions of dollars were at stake, entire industries waiting to be incorporated. Not to mention an underground arms race with China, Russia, and Brazil of all places.

Muongo could not believe what he was hearing. The whole business was an enormous racket run by a pack of bandits that were in a higher league than even the Four 'Yan Fashi. Mwizi was only trying to steal an election. They had stolen the future.

The undersecretary continued his droning recitation of the relevant laws and their penalties while Muongo watched the SUV's heavy tires slosh the residue of yesterday's snowsquall onto the wide sidewalks. The capital whirled past in a miasma of looming white pillars and marble slabs and black iron gates. He and Mwizi arrived in this city like two sharks in a pond of goldfish. They believed they would own every one of these buildings, and every decision made in them. After all, they had smashed all the rules they were supposed to have followed to get here. Turns out there are immutable rules, and bigger sharks. Mwizi had gone too far.

When they got into the building, the two men joined the Secretary of Defense who was sitting stone-faced in the hall outside the Oval Office door. The three men waited there in silence for over half an hour. Their audience with Mwizi would be less than two minutes.

Sasabonsam and a staff of four sat on the sofa. He gave whispered dictation to an aide typing furiously into a laptop. Mwizi was behind the big desk sipping a can of Diet Rite.

"Mr. President, you can't give the speech. You will be breaking a dozen laws."

Mwizi's glare latched onto Muongo. He ignored the two Pentagon men.

"Immunity," he mumbled. "Or have you already forgotten our little tea party with the Special Prosecutor last year?"

"But, sir, you will not be the only one at the podium. I'm delivering the FOIA section. Jack is doing the Florida thing."

"We'll come up with some bullshit. You'll be fine."

Jack, the Secretary of Defense, took one step toward the desk. "Sir, there is an executive order, signed by President Truman, that mandates silence."

"Oh yes, I've heard about that," he said with sudden interest. With a knuckle rap on his desktop, Sasabonsam glided across the room and set a paper before him, which he signed.

"I just rescinded it. Now, get the fuck out."

Door No. 2

8:23 P.M. EST

THE CIA DIRECTOR: Thank you, Mr. President.

For the next twenty years, sightings only increased, not just within U.S. airspace but all over the world.

This video was shot by the gun camera of a B-29 over the Gulf of Mexico on December 6, 1952. You see there a disc-shaped UFO circling the airplane. It then accelerated at 5,000 miles per hour toward a much larger "mother ship" that was over 150 feet in diameter. The two crafts converged and then departed the area at 9,000 miles per hour. The entire event was observed visually and tracked on radar. UFO maneuvers similar to this have been observed over Lake Huron, Goose Bay in Labrador, and Japan.

The Departments of Defense and Energy, with the support of CIA, worked diligently to discover the secret energy that powered the UFOs.

And then, in 1967, Congress passed and President Johnson signed the Freedom of Information Act. As well intentioned as it may have been, this disruptive law snarled the federal government in miles of red tape and put our national security at risk. In order to keep the UFO project from becoming known to our enemies, all UFO related research and technology was transferred to two private aerospace companies beyond the reach of that law.

This all-important project was locked away in sub-basements, and managed by small teams that were so compartmentalized and secretive they could not talk to one another, and in some cases did not even know of the other's existence. Under these conditions, the science work ground to a halt. The result is that we are no closer today to understanding what powers the UFOs, no closer to learning how to defend against them, than we were sixty years ago.

This is one of the reasons the president asked us to speak with you tonight. Eleven presidents before him fecklessly accepted the status quo. That ends tonight.

Late Saturday night, Sasabonsam hung upside down from a bar in his office closet doing stomach crunches. His goal was fifty reps. A motivational poster was pinned to the closet wall. It was an aerial photo of his artificial archipelago nation state. The nearly one thousand Clients pressed against the railings, waving at the sky. There were no words on this poster, but Sasabonsam could not look at it without recalling his original branding slogans. High Octane Freedom. Escape To The Future. Unleash Your Full Potential.

He had only visited his island nation once. On the one-year anniversary of its founding his private helicopter deposited him on the helipad to a hero's welcome. He gave a speech and accepted a trophy that the Clients had fashioned out of trash fished from the sea. His bags were packed for an overnight stay but as the dinner and celebration progressed he perceived that some strange political coalitions had formed in the Clients' first year, and that it might not be prudent for him to sleep there. Just before flying away, he told them they would give birth to a new type of human who would inherit the Earth one day. He believed it.

That was fourteen years ago. Those islands, along with many of the Clients, had long been at the bottom of the sea. Sasabonsam had always drawn inspiration from the fact that they were out there, even when they were eating each other. Perhaps especially then.

In the years since, he had put his efforts to the less audacious goal of turning America into that kind of place.

The section of the UFO speech on the national security state was a problem. Don't blow your wad all at once, Mwizi advised him. The paragraphs beautifully laid out the disadvantages of the military-industrial complex, and the solution of freeing it from all legal constraints was brilliant. It was also too much to hit the public with all at once. Privatizing the military and the intelligence agencies—that should come after inauguration, from the Blue Ribbon Commission Mwizi would convene and stack with all the right people.

Make UFOs the threat. Don't even hint at a policy idea that would give their enemies a hold.

He dropped from his bar and went to his desk. With a few clicks the paragraphs were copy-and-pasted into another file, awaiting future speeches. Then he made his way to the shower room in the basement.

Despite the late hour on a Saturday night, the office was fully staffed and bustling with preparations for the speech that would be delivered in less than twenty-four hours. The British ambassador was in the building making a last-ditch round of threats.

Clad in sweat-drenched shirt and shorts, Sasabonsam ignored everyone's stares as he hustled through the bullpen of cubicles and narrow hallways. He did his intense workout routine at the same hour every night, usually at an underground gym for practitioners of Silat martial arts on the east end of town. He only worked out in his office when he could not get away. And he had not been able to leave the White House grounds all week. He even slept on the couch in his office.

Since the transcript of his speech was spread around town, it seemed every spook in the field was lined up at the White House gate waiting for him to step outside. They were the gatekeepers of the government's UFO secrets, and they came one at a time, sometimes in pairs.

He was more annoyed than scared. For one, he was bulkier than most of them, and he was confident that his skills at Silat had attained deadly force, though he had not yet had the opportunity to test that confidence. Being able to fend off all comers with his fists had always been his motivation for the nightly workouts.

But he also smelled the agents' fear, and the fear of whoever sent them. Their front of cold confidence was flecked with desperation. Their dry script and shifting eyes showed them to be men who knew they were out of time and indecisive about whether or how to strike. This was Mwizi's doing. Everyone in the capital lived in fear of him. The select few who knew pieces of the truth about UFOs were in awe of the Four 'Yan Fashi. Others had come into this town hoping to do what they now threatened. No one had ever had the balls to pull the trigger.

The agents were professional, genteel in their gray government suits. Some pressured Sasabonsam to persuade Mwizi not to give the speech. Others threatened that he was going to be arrested and sent to Leavenworth for the rest of his productive years, or that he would simply be taken. Most of them just wanted to know how he had learned all the secrets that he had put in the speech. He must have some well-placed informants. For the good of national security, could he share some names?

Sasabonsam pitied these men for their ignorance. None of the agents actually knew the truth that was behind their questions. They could not imagine the enormity of what was about to happen. No one in a position to know had bothered to tell them. They were little more than drones.

The details of the speech had been in the public record for decades. They were not secrets at all, but scraps of the full, true story about UFOs that had been collected, indexed, archived, and stuffed into filing cabinets in the basements of eccentric hobbyists whom no one had ever paid any attention to except to mock.

Mwizi had only needed to declassify three lines of the twenty-seven-page speech. What made the speech dangerous was not its secret knowledge but the fact that it would be delivered from the White House Briefing Room above the seal of the President of the United States.

Sasabonsam had never thought about UFOs at all until one day, fourteen years earlier, he opened an email with a video attachment from a Client on his island. The video showed a blue-glowing triangle the size of a F-18 rising out of the ocean, hovering in the air while slowly rotating, and then accelerating out of sight in the blink of an eye. There was no doubt that it was real. He began reading every document he could find on what the eccentric hobbyists called the Phenomenon. He learned a great deal about what the triangle was, and other such craft.

But long before he read all the books and declassified reports, from the moment he saw the video, Sasabonsam knew that one day he would be in a position where it would pay enormous dividends to be able to tell the American people that their government has been lying to them about everything that mattered. That day had finally come.

On Tuesday all fifty states must certify their slate of electors for the presidential contest in order for Congress to include them to the vote tally the first week of January. On Monday the three Secretaries of State would announce they were declining to do so, citing evidence that their election integrity had been irreparably compromised. The UFO speech was set for Sunday night.

Door No. 3

8:47 P.M. EST
THE SECRETARY OF DEFENSE:

In the 1970s the United States installed in orbit the Defense Support Program satellite network, 21,000 miles above the surface of the Earth. It has served as an early-warning system capable of detecting missile launches on the ground. However, the infra-red sensors detect any object passing through orbit into United States territory. We have an analogous network, based on somewhat different detection methods, under the ocean.

The DSP system has detected many craft--almost too many to count--entering the atmosphere from deep space. There are a few spots on the globe where these craft then enter the oceans, where we believe they are concealing themselves in great numbers. One such landing spot is off the coast of Florida, east of Miami, north of Bermuda.

Here is a video of a UFO that passed between the DSP satellites and is seen transitioning from air into the water... Then the same craft or a similar one transitions from water to air...

Frankly, they're everywhere we look.

Deep in the sea between Georges Bank and Cape Cod, a Right Whale swam alongside an enormous, smooth disc that slowly rotated just above the muddy bottoms. She pressed her black, callosite-encrusted eye to the round porthole, which framed the whole body of her human friend. She asked why the voices had not laughed at her joke. She was miffed.

The Commander of the UFO assured her the joke was funny, but they could not be sure. He had a young daughter who subjected him to many jokes like that one, amalgamations of words that made no sense arranged in the cadence of a joke. With characteristic judiciousness the Commander conceded that his daughter was certainly laughing at something real that he could not hear. It was more likely that the whale's humor was lost in translation. Who were they to say it was not funny?

The joke was funny, the Commander reassuringly projected into the whale's mind.

Like his daughter, the whale insisted on a laugh. Having had much practice replying to a pantomimed joke with a pantomimed laugh, the Commander threw his head back and chortled while slapping his sides. Then they changed the subject.

How many calves last year?

The giant eye blinked. Forty-one, came the answer.

Excellent. Tell your pod to keep it up. Your descendants will thank you.

The UFO's clock, set to local time, chimed midnight. The long-awaited hour. It was time to go.

The Commander said goodbye, adding, *We will not meet again, but that is no reason not to keep working on your joke.*

The whale formulated a curse, which translated much more cleanly. After all, the greasy, reddish clumps of Right Whale poop produce an unmistakably noxious smell. Her body swung around and smacked the porthole with its tale, which sent the disc slowly careening toward the seafloor.

The tread of the Commander's boots gripped the deckplate until the anti-gravity field corrected for the tilt. As soon as the whale was a safe distance away, the same energy field sent the disc bobbing like a cork to the surface, and then shooting into the night sky.

The Commander remained at the porthole, watching the coastline twist beneath him like a dark ribbon.

***

In the capital, Mwizi turned off the TV and stepped outside. It was not to take in the crisp night air since the balcony was encased in bulletproof glass. He wanted to get a good look at the crowd, to hear their pitiful chants. They had been going all day and were running out of steam.

A sea of people stretched from the barricades on E Street across the Ellipse to the Mall. The mound around the Washington Monument was covered with an encampment of tents. The protestors' goal was to shame Congress into certifying the rightful winner of November's election, and the protest leaders vowed they would all stay until Mwizi was escorted out of the building on January 20th. Mwizi wanted to see if chanting was all they were prepared to do. With their voices going hoarse in the icy air, it would not be enough.

His faction in Congress was resolved, but the shaming had worked on the one person he needed to bring the plan home. When faced with his constitutional duty, stipulated by the 12th Amendment, to open and certify the Electoral College votes in the well of the House of Representatives, the vice president had choked. He resigned that morning and joined the enemy. As he pushed his letter across the desk, Mwizi's only reaction was to dictate a note to Sasabonsam. Never let him hire a Bible thumper for anything ever again.

The grandfather clocks in the center hall were still chiming midnight when he looked down from the balcony and noticed Ògbòó climbing into the black SUV. He watched the motorcade snake around the circular driveway on its way to the Capitol. Just before he left the residence, Ògbòó had resigned his speakership and his seat in Congress. In a few minutes he would be in the Senate, confirmed as the new vice president. And then, twelve hours later, he would preside over Mwizi's official reelection to a second term as President of the United States.

All the cogs were set in place, and the vast machinery of America's constitutional order clicked toward its last hour.

Mwizi dropped into the cushioned deckchair and threw up his legs. All day he had been watching his scheme play out on his TV, but the view through the plateglass, framed by the portico columns, was somehow better. This balcony now felt like the best seat in the house for the drama that was about to unfold.

He knew how the networks were framing the scene. News helicopters were filming Ògbòó's motorcade pull onto Pennsylvania Avenue, split screen with a tiny image of himself staring out at the protests.

When word spread through the crowd that Mwizi was on the balcony, the millions shifted on their little patch of grass trying to spy him out. Their chants intensified. Nearly every other American was at home in front of their TVs watching Mwizi look out at them. He could feel the frissive energy of all those eyes—and the strange impression that something else was watching him too.

It was Sasabonsam, of course. Always lurking. His hulking chief of staff had been leering through the door panes for some unknown number of minutes before stepping onto the balcony carrying a tray of Succulent. He sat in a patio chair beside Mwizi and raised one of the cartons in a toast.

Mwizi took a carton but waved off the gesture. He was not going to toast anything until Ògbòó was installed as his vice president. Until then, he was vulnerable.

"Suit yourself," Sasabonsam said. He raised his own green supplement drink to the sea of fist-pumping protestors and intoned, "To the end of the republic."

Mwizi twisted the cap and took a thirsty swig. "What the fuck is that supposed to mean? Who talks like that? This isn't a fucking Star Wars movie."

For weeks a constant audience of jawboning lawyers had paraded through the residence, counseling Mwizi on all the ways his plan to stay in power would end democracy as they knew it. He did not believe this. The election had in fact been stolen by the other guy, a bad, crooked man, and a Democrat. He was taking back what belonged to him.

But his pack of timid counselors kept coming, always launching the most boring debates imaginable about the features of a republic versus a democracy, and the arcane meanings of silly sounding Latin words. Every time they quoted Cicero, Mwizi reached for his remote.

The fact that he was able to extract from them the muddled conclusion that nothing he was doing was per se illegal, told him everything he needed to know about how the public would react. The protests would go on for a week, and then everyone would change the channel. After inauguration, all would carry on like normal. Just look at how they reacted to the UFOs.

Like a snake bite, the UFO speech stunned the body politic just long enough for the Four 'Yan Fashi to enact their plan. After Christmas, the realization set in that Mwizi had everything he needed to stay in power despite having lost the election. Half the country was filled with terror and rage, while the other half could not see why that distinction mattered. A split verdict. As Mwizi well knew, such verdicts accrue to the one playing offense.

The UFOs themselves slipped out of the public consciousness as dreams do. These mysterious craft receded back into their realm of unreality. Despite having read their descriptions from the teleprompter, Mwizi began to think it was bullshit. The last thing he expected was that one of them would actually show up.

It began as a point of light high in the southeast sky, brighter than the handful of stars whose billion-mile journey survived the city's haze. Brighter too than any planet. Mwizi had lived his entire life without knowing that five of the stars visible in the night sky were actually planets. Useless knowledge. Nor was he aware that the government had convinced generations of people who witnessed UFOs that what they actually saw was the planet Venus. In that, his ignorance was more common.

As the light swooped down and aimed directly for the building, what he thought he was looking at from his deckchair was a jet or helicopter. The only question in his mind was whether it was one of his own, or one commandeered by the enemy to take him out. If the latter, it was about to be blown out of the sky, to gouge a burning trench through the field of protestors. He grinned at the thought, and pitched forward to watch the show.

Instead, in the blink of an eye, the light expanded and came to an abrupt stop over the South Lawn. It was round, fifty feet across. Two convex discs of dull gray metal pressed together, tapering to a rounded edge that was ringed with glowing potholes brighter than magnesium flares.

A silhouette appeared in one of these portholes, and then passed through it on a beam of blue light that extended across the lawn. The blue beam gently deposited the reposed figure at the balcony's ledge. Here the figure stood erect and stepped across the gap of air. His body phased through the iron railings and the glass. His limbs and joints, the smooth flesh of his face vibrated where they made contact with these barriers.

Mwizi, still hunched over his knees, blinked to reset his vision on the blurring visitor. Once the Commander was standing on the balcony floor, there was nothing ghostly about him. Tall, powerfully built, unquestionably human. Dressed in a pale gray jumpsuit and black boots. He carried nothing in his hands. He had large, shimmering teeth like a game show host, pulled back in a merry smile.

As an experiment, Mwizi tossed his carton of Succulent at the visitor to see if he was solid. The carton struck his chest and splashed its green slime on the jumpsuit. Then came the voice.

Gentlemen, it is our honor to finally meet you.

The Commander's voice was deep and joyful, rumbling with a foreign but familiarly human dialect. It only existed as a gentle warbling within the forward portion of Mwizi's and Sasabonsam's brains.

Sasabonsam was so revolted by the violation that he jumped up, his body primed to attack. He knew it would be several crucial seconds more before the Secret Service agents could rush out from the hall, and minutes before backup could arrive.

As a courtesy, the Commander let the first punch land on his solar plexus, but he blocked every other blow. This only made Sasabonsam more enraged. His fists, feet, knees, and elbows flailed with the deadly force he had always wanted to unleash on another person, but the Commander's gliding parries channeled that energy back.

Mwizi, who always made a point to watch the Saturday afternoon Kung-Fu movie, was almost entertained by the display. Since his youth, his physical cowardice had kept him out of the actual fist fights that tended to erupt around him. His only skill in a fight was to take instant measure of an opponent. So he thought it rather stupid to attack a man who could walk through walls. He did nothing to pull back his chief of staff.

Wielding a blur of forearm blocks and confident footwork, the Commander walked Sasabonsom backward around the crescent of the balcony toward the residence. With one final, little jab, he knocked Sasabonsam through the open door into Mwizi's living room. He then shifted his weight, leaning steeply to catch the lower edge of the wide French door with the toe of his boot. In one fluid movement, his leg swept in the opposite direction, pulling the door closed.

As the Commander's extended leg progressed along this arc, his body, the door, Sasabonsam's screams, and everything else that was in motion began to drag at an unnatural rate of speed. With unbearable slowness the door whooshed into its frame and the handle clicked into its latch, and Time itself seemed to stop entirely.

Door[3]

Early in the Commander's training, when he was little more than a boy, the elders took him into the southern savannas to hunt a lion that had acquired the taste for human flesh. When they cornered it in the rock outcrop, the creature paced and stomped the dirt. Its roars were meek, like it knew the game was up. It was a scrawny, unwell, crazed shell of its regal kind. The elders pushed him forward, gun in hand, his eyes brimming with reverence, love, purpose, and no trace of sorrow. The Commander had the same look in his eye now as he turned to face Mwizi.

Mwizi surveyed this new environment. It felt like someone had paused the movie. He was still on the balcony, seated comfortably. At his feet was the carton of Succulent tipped over in a green puddle. The UFO still hovered down the lawn. The millions of protestors were still lined up at his fence, but now they were perfectly still and silent. That whatever had happened had finally plugged up their pathetic chants amused him and provoked an involuntary laugh. The laugh moved in his lungs but made no sound. There was no sound anywhere.

It was not the case that there was no movement. A Black Hawk helicopter had been on a flight path swooping between the balcony and the UFO. It hung in the air, nose down, just above the treetops to Mwizi's left. He could see the marines hanging out the open door staring at him. The four rotary blades still turned but almost imperceptibly, a bit faster than the minute hand of a clock.

Mwizi looked to his new, unexpected enemy. The Commander's form shimmied again like it had when it passed through the glass, and he came back to life. His heavy shoulders swung around. The smile returned to his lips. As he walked back across the balcony, a faded echo of his body remained at the door facing Sasabonsam. The voice returned to Mwizi's head.

As we were saying, sir, we have been looking forward to this meeting for a long time.

Mwizi could not think what to say. His thoughts were tangled with unformed questions so that no complete thought could form—though not so many questions as a more curious person might have had if they were in the same position. He picked the most direct one that might extract himself from this negotiation, where he had the upper hand in nothing.

Though his mouth moved, there was still no sound. With a little practice he learned to focus his speech into thoughts like the Commander.

What do you want?

The Commander was not surprised by Mwizi's incuriosity. By his clock, there was time enough for a bit more conversation than that.

Only to help, the Commander replied with a voice that was as warm as his smile. *We began visiting your world in great number in 1945. By coincidence, the year of your birth. Our vessels are equipped to intercept and disarm your nuclear weapons in the event of a war. You may be surprised to know that we have done so three times in your history. A mishap on a Soviet submarine. An accident in an Arkansas silo that caused a missile to explode. A skirmish that escalated out of control on the India-Pakistan border.*

Mwizi shrugged. *No nukes here.*

The Commander mirrored Mwizi's unmoving stare, waiting.

Why would aliens give a shit if we blow each other up? Not your planet.

Do we look alien to you?

You look like some thug from Baltimore.

The Commander laughed heartily. *And we are honored to be mistaken for one. The descendants of your Stolen Ones are sacred to us.*

The Commander waved his arm toward the UFO.

Vessels such as this, which have been seen in your skies for generations, are not crewed by aliens. They are not spaceships. They are time machines. Far in your future, that vessel will be built in our Johannesburg shipyard. Its crew is from many places, towns and villages across Africa and South America.

He placed his hand to his heart. *I am from Congo, and will be born in a city that will not be built for many centuries.*

His gesture toward the UFO put the frozen sea of people in the Commander's field of view for the first time. He had known they would be there, and the waves of emotion that his training had prepared him for began to pool in his eyes. With his back to Mwizi, he stepped close to the glass, trying to discern a face. All of them upturned, gleaming in the blazing white light of the UFO. They were ghosts of their future selves.

The people in the protest crowd had no part to play in the Commander's mission, but in the aftermath of it they would become the most important people in the history of the world. Each of them would spend the rest of their lives—blessed long lives—telling the story of when the UFO landed at the White House. The name of the park or the street they were standing in, and of the people they were with, would be in their mouths, freshly remembered, until their last day on Earth.

Millions died, millions sickened, many children unborn in the three events we told you of, the Commander explained as he continued to gaze into the crowd. *At each juncture when we reset the past, we looked forward in the hope that the conflagration would not occur. But it does, each time.*

There will be a full-scale nuclear war. All nations that possess the terrible weapons will use them. Billions of people will die horribly. Earth's biome will be radically altered. The northern hemisphere will become an irradiated wasteland. Enough people in the south will survive. People from places that the superpowers did not deem worthy targets.

Mwizi snorted. *You're telling me that Africans invented time travel.*

Well, broadly speaking, the team was from all reaches of the continent, but the woman who solved the key engineering challenges was from Uganda.

That's the stupidest fucking then I've ever fucking heard. How?

One step at a time, as with anything.

Mwizi's brow scrunched. *Do you mean, like, nigger Africans or Planet of the Ape Africans?*

The Commander turned from the glass and loomed over his mark. *In our world, your total ignorance is the stuff of legends and bedtime stories. To be face-to-face with it, takes the breath away.*

This, a statement of fact rather than an insult, delivered by someone whose childhood, thousands of years from now, was to be filled with stories wherein Mwizi is chief king of all the monsters of mythology ancient and future, would have given a person with normally balanced emotions a moment's pause to question their life choices. To Mwizi it registered not at all. The only time scale he cared about were the votes about to happen in Congress. The helicopter's blades had not completed one rotation. Sasabonsam was still reaching for the doorknob. At this rate, it would take years before he would be voted president.

Can't you come back tomorrow? Say three o'clock. I'll be in a better position to negotiate terms.

The Commander made a sympathetic frown. *No time, I'm afraid. The nuclear holocaust we are here to stop will occur during your second term as president.*

Mwizi's telepathic yippie was so exuberant it made the Commander flinch. *Hot damn. So it's going to work.* He pointed toward the Capitol. *My man in the car right now.*

The Commander laughed, and the broad smile returned to his lips. *Our elders bid us read our Shakespeare, and praise God they did. It makes this era sensible to us.*

Whatever—wait, you're saying I start a nuclear war?

Oh my, yes. You are doing it right now. You see, at each of the three junctures when we reset the past, we looked forward in the hope that the final conflagration would not occur. We are by nature an optimistic people, and we had an optimistic theory. The reason your great powers saw fit to choose total war with nuclear weapons was because you had tasted those three nuclear disasters and survived them with a manageable loss of life. This was forbidden knowledge you should not have had. Swiping it from your history and your memory would restore the natural state of fear and mystery that protects us all from mass death. But each time, you and your three 'Yan Fashi show up and lay waste to our petty hopes and dreams.

So I'm important?

Mmhmm. And constant as the northern star.

The Commander lowered himself into the patio chair, spread his arms wide, and told the end of story as it had been told to him, as he had told his daughter. This would be the last time telling it.

When you ended democracy in America, it broke the world's heart. No one believed in anything. Everyone became a killer. Their deep anger and hatred became a weariness. So very tired. When the nuclear weapons were used, it was not because of any accident or tragic series of unforeseen escalations. They wanted their world to burn.

Mwizi tracked the Commander's sweeping hands as each word dropped into his mind. He sensed, but did not recognize, that these words described the true contours of his own empty soul. Within that shell, the frail little slug that was his conscience recoiled at being seen and caused Mwizi's whole body to shudder and jump out of the chair.

With the danger of self-revelation pushed away, all Mwizi knew for sure was that the world the Commander had described was the one he wanted to live in, apart from the mass death of course.

He also knew that despite whatever magic trick was slowing the flow of time, if he wanted to stay in that world and remain its master, he only had a few moments left to close the most important deal of his life.

So his lanky body jerked around, his legs dancing like a spark. He felt good, alive with more vitality than had coursed through his thin, frail limbs in a long time. Looming above the Commander's intrigued gaze, with his arms out, caressing the air, Mwizi made his pitch.

You want peace on Earth, I'll do peace. I'll get rid of all our nukes. I can do anything you like. I'm about to be elected president.

But you're not.

Mwizi's hands dropped. *Bullshit. You just said it. My vice president is about to certify my win.*

The Commander flicked his brow toward the driveway. *He's not your vice president yet. And I'm afraid traffic on Pennsylvania Avenue is moving frightfully slow.*

The brief flicker of liveliness left Mwizi's body. His shoulders slouched.

You're taking me, aren't you?

The Commander's smile widened as he nodded.

Mwizi's feet lifted off the balcony tiles. The beam of blue light that had delivered the Commander from the UFO now enveloped him. The weightlessness made his stomach churn.

We are going to take a quick spin around the Earth. You and I will both get one last look. Meanwhile, your Congress is already evacuating the city. By the time the sun rises: No president. No vice president. No speaker of the house. The chief justice will be rushed to the bunker where the pro tempore of the Senate is hiding and deliver the oath of office.

The light pulled Mwizi backward. The spot where his back bumped into the plateglass disintegrated into a kind of physical static that expanded and tickled his skin as he passed through it. Uncanny as this was, he was in no way distracted from the endgame that the Commander just spelled out for him.

But... he's a Democrat, Mwizi bellowed. *That's not fair. He's damn near one hundred years old. He thinks I'm his Uncle Jethro. You can't put him in charge.*

It's only for three weeks. During which time Congress will have a change of heart and certify the democratically elected winner of your most recent election.

Despite the tingling paralysis spreading from his immobile core into his appendages, and his body suspended midway through the circle of frizzing glass, Mwizi lunged at the Commander. His arms flailed about until his hands found a solid edge of glass. Pulling with all his strength, he momentarily slowed his extraction by the light.

Wait, he pleaded, trying to reason. *If you stop the nuclear war, won't Africa turn back into a shithole in your time?*

The Commander again laughed at the pitiful ignorance. But he knew that the temporal mechanics suggested by Mwizi's question was broadly correct.

It is true. Once you leave this timeframe, everyone from our world will cease to exist.

Mwizi smacked both hands against the glass, certain he had found his out. *Then why are you doing this?*

Ùbúnt'ù

We don't speak shithole here. This is the White House.

Ùbúnt'ù is our faith in human singularity. If our neighbor needs something we have, we freely give it to them. We do this because we and they are the same person, the same manifestation of the mind of God.

The Commander motioned to the people on the Ellipse. *They are our neighbors. What they need is more life, and we have life in abundance. So here we are.*

Mwizi could not understand. This is no way mattered. He was moments away from experiencing the connectivity of all life and matter in the universe on the subatomic level. The pull of the light increased, plucking him through the glass.

We're not even your people, he screamed so shrilly the Commander winced.

And for many years that was debated in our counsels. The tipping point was the descendants of the Stolen Ones, nearly all killed in your war. We felt we owed a special debt to them.

Snared within the light, Mwizi's supine body stopped thrashing. His telepathic screams quieted in the Commander's mind and became the first sounds to rush back into the vacuum of silence. Propelled by vocal cords now rather than mere thought, their fury pealed through the night.

The further Mwizi receded into the blinding light of the UFO, the more time accelerated toward its petty pace. The helicopter drifted in front of the balcony. Sasabonsam unlatched the door, and Secret Service agents ambled into the living room.

The Commander slid off the cushions to his knees. He mumbled a prayer in his true voice. He blessed his ancestors, both those who lived and were yet to be born. He thanked the elders who had prepared him for this day.

To ensure that their mission was complete, he searched for the dark spot in the light. Mwizi, the Great Thief, floated over the lawn. His back was arched, his long arms and legs dangling, looking just like the scrawny lion of his youth being hauled out of the savanna on a pallet. Just as an ember of sympathy was catching in his heart, the scene reminded him of a line from one of the plays the elders had made them read.

"Fair is foul and foul is fair," he whispered, his breath fogging the glass encasement. "Hover through the fog and filthy air."

By the time Sasabonsam reached the deckchair, he was alone. The UFO was still over the lawn. Its lights had blinked out. He could hear the president's howls of rage and pain. They bleated echo-like across a vast, unbridgeable canyon.

The dark gray disc wafted sideways over the masses, hung there above their upturned faces for a moment, and then shot straight up and out of sight. It sliced through the stratosphere, the thermosphere, punching through the sky's utmost balcony into the inky black of space. It was still night.

Here the craft turned on its edge and rocketed along the arc of Earth's orbit. When it hit the sunrise, its skin turned the color of lightning. Tomorrow was dawning, and each of the billion rays of sunshine sloughed off its bounty of atoms, exploding each electron bond and sending its energy back into the cosmic wellspring.

Mwizi found himself standing alone in the hollow core of the craft. None of his five human senses seemed to be connected to his body any longer, but he did sense metal warping, spewing unbearable heat—not only that, but the fabric of the universe itself dissolving around him.

For some unfixed spell of time, his consciousness was all that remained. And at the very moment when that bare essence transubstantiated into nothingness, he felt a sensation even more foreign and strange—a wonderful feeling, one that he had been seeking his entire life. Never found, until he found himself here in the empty solitude of oblivion. Happiness.

| 3 |

Four Conversations

Muroc Airfield, Pancho's Bar (interior) - sometime next year

The TV blared like it was the end of the whole goddamn world. For Stephanie Jones it was worse than that. The studio had pulled the plug on her movie hours before she was to start filming. All because of the indescribable bullshit on the TV.

Her phone was blowing up too, texts and calls. She'd been working it since the news came, trying to salvage what was left of her life. Now, as she slid into the last seat at the bar, in what felt like an unrecoverable act of rebellion for the three seconds it took to press the buttons down, she turned the phone off. The righteous satisfaction she'd expected to find reflected back from the dead screen never came. Rebellion against what? The people who mattered were not the ones trying to reach her. Stephanie slammed the slab face down on the bar with a force intended to crack it to shards. There wasn't anyone left on the planet she wanted to talk to.

There was one person she had to talk to, and she was on her way.

As if on cue, the barkeep slid before her. A pile of blond hair wrapped up in a bandana, bright red lipstick, breasts up and out and framed in lace. Like any good barkeep, her eyes turned down to match the sorrow they read in her customer's. Her round face held a thin, sad smile.

Stephanie did not make eye contact, but asked for the real stuff from the bottle they'd been saving for after the shoot. Pancho twirled around. She riffled through the rows of mostly Mexican hooch lined up against the wall until she found the tall, square bottle of bourbon.

As she poured, her southern California accent came out of another century. "Oh hon, you sure screwed the pooch on this one. They'll be another one."

Stephanie drank first and then flashed her bugeyed *What the fuck?* look.

Pancho poured another and pointed the bottle neck to one of the picture frames on the wall. "This reminds me of the time this ace I once dated up and went cross eyed during an inverted roll. Just bad luck."

Stephanie wasn't sure if she was trying to be kind or mean. She wasn't done.

The barkeep leaned back against the counter, elbows planted, and looked up at all the black and white photographs that covered the wall from the bottles of hooch clear to the ceiling.

"Sometimes I stare at these faces and I wonder. What's the difference between the ones who got to walk away, go back to their pretty little wives, and the ones who got mushed into creamed corn on the desert floor?"

Stephanie did not feel like she had walked away from this one. She had screwed the pooch, but good. She realized that her body was still in shock from the hit. Two shots of bourbon did not taste like anything and had no effect at all. Her first movie was an indie that she'd made for less than $750,000. The studio plucked her out of a Sundance awards lineup, gave her $165 million and told her to make it her way. It should not have happened, and it would not happen a second time. She'd picked the wrong script. The last thing she wanted to do was sulk about it with Pancho Barnes.

The director flashed her fake smile at the barkeep, adding, "How about you take the rest of the night off."

Pancho threw her head back, chortling.

Seeing her only barfly was in no mood to talk, Pancho poured one more and left the bottle as directed. She joined the rest of her customers, who were squeezed around the corner table. Someone had pulled over a monitor so they could all watch the president's presentation.

The bar was a perfect scene setter. All red brick and old timbers, cracked by sun and packed with dust from the California desert. An old upright piano that had the dust knocked out of it every night. A long wraparound bar top that was solid wood and polished. The framed pictures of pilots. The two dudes with buzzcuts milling about in the corner, dressed in khakis and checkered shirts, spitting images of Chuck Yeager and Neil Armstrong.

There was a ragged screen door and porch that framed the desolate patch of earth where the bar was embedded like a tick amid alfalfa scrub and Joshua trees. Beyond the line of cottonwoods and poplars that fenced Pancho's little oasis was the great flat blasted white expanse of Rogers Dry Lake, and the airfield where the planes took off, landed, and sometimes turned their pilots into creamed corn. The sky was empty now and silent, purplish going black. The sunbaked flats glowed like bone in the moonlight.

It was out of this celestial aura that Dee exuded. She climbed the steps and lingered on the other side of the screen, unsure she'd come to the right place. She looked lost in more ways than one.

Stephanie did not call her over right away. She needed a moment to get straight in her head what she was supposed to say and not say. Her day had started that morning, before everything else went to shit, with a call from Dee's husband, Craig. He told her that Dee had recently been diagnosed with early onset dementia. Don't talk to her about it, he said. Just be aware. Be a friend.

Stephanie's first thought was about the movie. It would not be a problem for production. The script was delivered, and the less writers hung around after that the better. It was just sad. Dee had an uncommon mind. An accomplished astronomer. A director of SETI. She was the rarest of birds, a woman popularizer of science. For years before Stephanie came to town, Dee had dropped in and out of Hollywood to make her documentaries. *Starcatcher* was her first movie script, and it all but guaranteed her a second career as a screenwriter if she wanted. It was that good.

Worse, in their ten months together blocking the story and putting the script together, Stephanie had decided against all her instincts that she liked Dee. They were both hard and exacting. Dee called her girlfriend and made no end of inappropriate salt and pepper jokes. Stephanie would not go so far as to call her a friend, but she was sad for her.

When Dee spotted Stephanie, she finally pushed through the screen door. "Help me, Stephanie," she pleaded. "I do not understand what is happening."

"The studio pulled the movie. We're out of a job."

"But everything is ready. You were filming today."

"Yeah, well, I guess they figured, people already weren't going to movies, and after today, they ain't never going back. Especially to see our kind of movie. I'm sorry, Dee."

Anger flared. "Don't you dare apologize to me. I'm an old woman. I wrote it as a lark. But you. This was..."

Stephanie poured for herself, knowing Dee had no taste for alcohol. She swiveled her back to the rest of the bar and slouched over the counter, sipping more slowly.

She could taste the bourbon now, and the grief. Her mind reeled. No woman had ever been handed the keys to a summer sci-fi blockbuster, let alone one with her skin tone and her cast. Stephanie always suspected that some of the smiling faces around the big table believed her movie would flop, even secretly desired that it would, she just didn't know how many. Since you never know how many there are, it is always safer to assume that it's all of them.

They approved it only because there was not one racial note in the whole movie. Its tone was universal. Dee was the whitest person Stephanie had ever met, but her script was not. Maybe because it was set so far in the future, the humans in the story all had bigger things to think about.

In the corner someone turned up the TV, which reminded Stephanie that now they all had bigger things to think about too.

Dee patted her back. "What are you going to do?"

"Maybe Beyonce will throw me a music video when she hits her afro-futurism phase. Consolation prize."

She felt Dee's thin arms wrap around her shoulders and squeeze, which caused her whole body to stiffen.

"Kubrick. There was one slick motherfucker. Slicker than me. He foresaw this."

Stephanie was trying to sour her, and it worked. Dee retracted her embrace and crinkled her nose. "You know that movie is gibberish to me. And too much. Just too much. I don't understand it."

During their process, Stephanie talked a lot about *2001: A Space Odyssey*, making Dee watch it multiple times. At the climax of the movie, the big reveal, the camera spins around to show the camera crew filming the whole thing. Baller move, Stephanie would say. She was a three-picture deal away from the suits letting her get away with a shot like that.

Stephanie reached down the bar and slid a thick bound stack of white pages between them—the shooting script. "This was my launch pad. What did I do? Screwed the fucking pooch. What did Kubrick do? That motherfucker dialed up Lloyd's of London and took out alien insurance. He literally got on the phone with the number one insurance broker in the world and asked to take out insurance on the off chance that aliens would land on the fucking Earth. Why? Because he knew that if the UFOs revealed themselves before his release date it would kill all the buzz for his movie. That motherfucker knew how to sweat the details."

The crinkle in Dee's nose spread to her eyebrows.

More people pushed into the barroom. On the TV, the president began his speech. He was standing on a stage in the maw of an enormous Air Force hangar. Behind him, shimmering against the blue sky, was a giant triangle floating just off the tarmac. It was silver, reflecting sunlight like a mirror. The only marking, the only recognizable human thing on it, was the black, gray, and blue seal of the United States Space Command.

It was above this airfield, on October 14, 1947, the president began his remarks, *when Chuck Yeager did what so many believed he could not do. A plane that could break the sound barrier could not be built. That's what people said. But American engineers and American pilots knew better. Today, this generation of engineers and pilots have done the impossible yet again...*

Dee turned from the TV. She folded her arms on the counter to steady herself, but her eyeballs twitched back and forth. Quietly, desperately, she pleaded, "I do not understand what is happening."

Stephanie was careful. By now, everyone in the world understood what was happening. She had never dealt with dementia before.

During their time working together, Dee had become slower to speak, like she was collecting her thoughts word by word. She would become uncharacteristically cranky, even mean. She would get these looks, like she just turned a corner onto an unfamiliar street and was mentally retracing her steps back. The deep look of loss on her face now was different. It had less to do with the plaques building up on her myelin and the atoms of consciousness slowly sloughing off into oblivion. It was more of a professional shock. In the span of a few hours, her entire cosmology had been blasted out an airlock.

Stephanie spit out the news of the day as quickly as she could. "A hundred years ago a flying saucer crashed in the desert—just like they always told us never happened. They kept it a secret until they figured out how to back-engineer the technology, and now Uncle Sam has an anti-gravity flying machine. End of fucking story."

Dee's look of loss only furrowed, as though she did not understand a word of what Stephanie just said. "What does any of that have to do with us?"

"You mean our movie?" Stephanie began flipping open pages. "You wrote a space opera that is obsessed with being true to known science. All of the true-to-life details are what drew me to it. Action sequences dictated by the ruthless clockwork of physics. Not a single detail for Neil deGrasse Tyson to bitch about on his socials. It reads like a Jules Verne novel."

"Now, there is a writer who makes sense," Dee cooed.

"Yes, he does. Exquisite common sense." The director folded the script open to the page she would have been shooting right now instead of having this excruciating conversation. "Scene 1: Muroc airfield. The first people skim the edge of space in their experimental jet planes. Yeager in the X-1. Armstrong is here too, scheduled to go up fifty miles in the X-15, break through the thin brown line that separates the air we breathe from starlight. Nevermind that Armstrong did not come to Muroc until 1960, and Pancho's burned to the ground in 1953. Let no man countermand the law of mass-ratios. But history, that is fungible, because who the fuck knows what really went down, and the audience doesn't give two shits to begin with."

The director flipped more pages. "Planes that are fueled by alcohol and liquid oxygen. Spacecraft with hydrogen-peroxide thrusters. Which is fine, because it is 19-40-fucking-7. But then—" She flopped to the start of Act II. "—one hundred years later, to the day I might add—" She jabbed a thumb over her shoulder at the TV. "—we should have gotten gigs as presidential script writers instead of the hacks that wrote this shit—" She spread her hand over the page. "—you have the first human interstellar voyage, and it's a rocket no bigger than the Atlas. Sure it's nuclear powered, but it's still a length of pipe spitting fire out its ass."

Dee shrugged her *don't-blame-me* shrug, which Stephanie had gotten to know very well. "That's just how it would be done."

"Their descendants end up populating the entire galaxy, which is empty, I might add. Not one alien in the entire movie, which, as you recall, we had to fight for. Our interstellar ship spends six pages of script getting to the nearest star, but in story time, 20,000 years. And then, once they plant their colony, do they venture forth to the next star system? No they do not. They wait, pages and pages of waiting, until the galaxy's fluid movements bring the star to them, which takes another 100,000 years."

The shrug again, and a weary, cold eye. "Interstellar travel at a smaller time scale is impractical."

Stephanie plopped the script open to the last scene. She made no attempt to reign in her exasperation. "And for the grand finale, our AI descendants, which inhabit enormous solar-system spanning crystalline bodies, construct a Rube Goldberg device out of black holes, which they use to lasso all the galaxies, reverse the slow, spreading-out death of the universe by pulling all of creation into an equilibrium where dark energy and gravity are precisely balanced."

"Everything consistent with the cosmological model as we understand it."

"That's the problem. Your cosmological model went out the window at nine o'clock this morning."

The lost look returned to Dee's face.

Stephanie closed the script and pushed it toward her.

"It's cold, lifeless, joyless."

"So is the universe."

"That was its charm. Your ideas were interesting enough, and fuck all else. Your conviction is what held the script together. There is just one problem. You were wrong about everything. One day we will be able to lasso a galaxy, but someone else can't come here in a UFO?"

"No, no, no."

Stephanie laughed and signed all at once. "You sound crazy, Dee. You are the kook now."

On the TV, a line of pilots in blue jumpsuits had gathered underneath the floating triangle. Two of the pilots climbed a ladder to the small bubble cockpit on the top. Stephanie swiveled Dee's barstool around and made her look at them.

"See those red-blooded American flight jocks—and the one pretty little white girl—good for her—that is who people will want to see a movie about. Won't even need the movie. Just turn on the news. They will be showing who's who over the South China Sea by dawn's early light. Before the year is out, they'll be on Alpha Centauri."

Stephanie saw the anger rising on Dee's pink face. She splashed the bourbon in a glass, then splashed a little more, and pushed it toward her hands. Dee sipped.

Dee was a graduate student in 1977 when the Wow! Signal was detected. An alien civilization living close to the galactic core had built an enormous transmitter, pointed it toward the Orion Arm, and blasted the Earth with radio waves for 72 seconds—that's what she wanted to believe back before quaint notions like wanting to believe something were swiped from her programing. The signal was so extremely powerful and non-random that it leapt out from the galactic background radiation. The astronomer who first spotted the signal zipping across the computer printout scrawled Wow! in the margin. But because the anomalous artifact never repeated, it could not be sufficiently studied to the point where astronomers were comfortable settling on a judgment as to what it was. Dee became so fascinated by the idea that no one could prove it had not come from aliens that she set out to prove it was. She spent a year of her dissertation on it, until the astronomy chair convinced her to scrap her thesis and turn it into a very interesting, very mundane study of the refractive properties of cosmic dust. In the '90s she was part of Project META. For five years, radio telescopes scanned the entire northern sky searching for an alien signal in the watering hole frequency. The conventional wisdom had always been that out of all the radio frequencies on the dial, the aliens would call us using the narrow band in the electromagnetic spectrum, between 1420 and 1662 megahertz, where there is the least amount of interstellar background noise. The team detected 37 candidate signals. Like the Wow! Signal, all originated from the galactic plane, were inexplicable, and did not repeat. It was thrilling work, but nothing came of it. Except that Spielberg had partially funded META, and afterward helped Dee get her start in the documentary business.

After META, the prickly sense that she had wasted her career began a long, slow ascent through her subconscious. Something was not right. Humans start playing around with radio telescopes in 1937, and 23 years later have a Eureka! moment where they realize the one way aliens will communicate with us is through a complex and mind-bogglingly expensive device that would feed directly into our radio telescopes. It was anthropomorphic silliness. When this little burr of truth finally bobbed to the surface, she picked it up and pressed it into her heart, relishing the pain. The galaxy was a lifeless place, but it did not need to be forever. *Starcatcher* was her coming out, a final break from her professional life. Not that this would prove controversial in her circles. Like good scientists, her colleagues entertained the possibility before retreating to the comforting statistic that only a small percent of the sky had been heard from. It was only a movie after all, they would no doubt say. Once production wrapped, she would resign from SETI, and spend the required weeks doing promotions. Dee was tired of asking the questions. She was ready to turn away from the void. But somewhere along the way the void had thrust into her.

Over the last ten months, as she wrote the script, the fuzzy emptiness had jumped from her telescope lens inside her own head. It was on the edges, but she could sense it rolling imperceptibly toward the core of her consciousness. The background static was coming for her. She had been staring into the stars too long.

Dee had only vaguely understood what Stephanie had been explaining. It fell on her ears as flat as Hollywood talk. Then the TV network's space-science reporter—a man she knew—said something that caught her ear.

"What year did he say?"

Stephanie had been listening intently to the reporter's recounting of the story. "1948," she said without looking away from the screen. "I guess that's when they found it. On a mesa in New Mexico. God, what a great MacGuffin. I already know how it's going to be. They'll give it to Spielberg. They'll trot Lucas out of retirement. One big, happy

American adventure story. Nolan will cut a bitch. Maybe I can wrangle a spot as an assistant."

The number Stephanie had just given, Dee carefully turned over and over in her mind. The flashes of rage that came from nowhere, which had been an increasingly frequent symptom of her condition, flared within her now.

"I'm so angry, I could just scream."

When Dee tried it, the scream did not come out satisfactorily. Her yip was not enough to draw the attention of any of the others in the bar who were fixated on the TV. This added embarrassment to her inchoate rage. She picked up her glass and threw it against the wall. That was better. A slew of bottles and three picture frames skittered to the floor and shattered.

"How could they do this to us? These men in Washington. It's a crime. Unforgivable. Evil."

Stephanie's attention was also now sucked into the TV, where the silver triangle was flitting about over the desert—the most compelling piece of film she had ever seen. The camera would occasionally return to the smiling faces of the men from Washington. Politicians. Military. Bureaucrats. Some of them looked quite old—the functionaries who hatched this enormous lie, who nurtured it, kept it going year after year. Stephanie grew up in D.C. Her family had lived there since slave days. Her mother grew up in a row house and could see the Capitol dome when sitting on the fence in the backlot. Stephanie knew better than to be surprised by the perfidy of these men, or to expect retribution. Her answer to Dee's question came slow, without taking her eyes off the screen. "They're going to dazzle us with bullshit until we forget about that part."

But Dee had already climbed down from the barstool and wandered out the screen door. Her gaze swept across the bone-white lake bed covered in a crystalline moonlight. The Joshua trees stalked across the desert like an army of alien skeletons. An eerie, diffuse red glow undulated above the western mountains. She shivered and wrapped her shawl about her.

Dee was still trying to count down from the number. She had worked with much bigger numbers, yet this one was giving her trouble. She hoped it was the bourbon, but suspected it was not.

Stephanie's thick boot tread creaked onto the porch steps.

"Eight," she whispered. "Eight decades. So much started right here. Just imagine the world we'd be living in today if they had only told us the truth."

Stephanie thought Dee looked like she needed a hug. Stephanie did not do hugs, but for once she knew the right thing to say. "I don't have to. You wrote it."

Dee almost said aloud—she almost even admitted it to herself—she felt glad to be losing her mind.

Stephanie jumped down. She reached into the periphery. Her fingers wrapped around the mountains and pushed. The matte painting slid aside, revealing the studio's back wall, and a metal door beneath a red EXIT sign.

The women said goodbye. Stephanie offered to drive her in a cart to the parking lot, but Dee declined. She knew the way.

The director stayed in the studio. She walked a hundred yards from the Pancho's Bar set to where the spaceship sat on a gimbaled floor. It was long, smooth, and gleaming white, separated into three pieces for interior and exterior shooting. She stepped inside, clomped down the glassy corridors, and dropped into the cockpit seat. A sweeping, empty bay window, backed by bluescreen, was before her. The control panels, the deckplates, the seat upholstery were all as richly and lovingly detailed as the barroom, but to Stephanie it just felt like the day job she'd been fired from. She'd overseen every inch of it rendered and constructed, and all that mattered to her was the light sources and the camera mounts. Her imagination had inhabited this little ship for countless hours as she had planned out and second guessed her angles, her close ups, her wide shots. There was no magic to it, just the shooting schedule, a marathon of takes, six grueling months. Her toe had been poised on the starting line, her mind and body focused, just as the ground was yanked out from underfoot.

It occurred to her that she will never be here again. She will never be the person that she was that morning. Forget clawing back her prestige. Even if they let her do another movie—about anything, space travel or medieval knights—nothing will ever be the same. All the old stories feel hollow. The world before today, our lives in it and the lives of our ancestors, none of it is what we thought it was. There will need to be new stories, which is the one thing—the only thing—that no one in this town knows how to do. It is not their job. Might as well shut it down, turn off the lights.

As she stared into the blue, all the disconnected scenes, all the technical bits meshed together. Stephanie realized how much she had been looking forward to seeing the finished product on the big screen. The premier was going to be glorious. The opening scene hove into view of her mind's eye. She slumped low in the chair, propped her boots on the console, and let her gaze melt into the bluescreen. The whole movie exuded out of her mind. It flowed scene after scene, without her having to think or consciously remember. It was as her audience would have experienced it, without the specter of the camera. She let it play until the credits.

When she came out of this trance, Stephanie had no idea how long she had been sitting inside the darkened spaceship. The overhead lights in the bay had been turned on, and workers were circling, prying apart panels and beams with crowbars and hammers. Everything would be gone by morning. She remembered the bourbon and sprinted back to fetch the bottle.

When she finally made it to the parking lot she was surprised to find Dee still there. Her slight, stooped frame was swaying eerily under a lamppost. Stephanie walked quietly to her car and opened the door. It was dark and Dee was several rows away. She wanted nothing more than to go home and be alone for the next six months, and she would have done just that if Craig had not called her that morning.

Dee looked startled, not recognizing the tall, broad shape of her friend until Stephanie stepped into the circle of light. "I've lost my keys," she said with a catching tremor in her voice.

Stephanie swiveled around. It was hopeless to look. The keys could be anywhere on the lot. "Come on, I'll give you a lift to your hotel."

"No," Dee insisted icily. "They're right here. I know it."

"All right," Stephanie said placidly.

Each took a position on the opposite edge of the light. Heads down, they paced the circle, working their way to the center.

Palmdale, California – 1984

Peter Morgan fell in love with a boy in seventh grade and never quite fell out. Tom Osberg was his best friend. They were always together. The kind of friends who every time they would pass in the hall, or convene at their lockers, would huddle for some urgent, shorthand conversation and then peel away to act on the shared intelligence, like pubescent business partners. They bonded over all the same things boys their age were doing—weekend games of penny-ante poker, catching *Star Trek* reruns whenever they were on, sailing on the Sound—but it was on Scout trips when Peter began to feel that first flush of a deeper kind of love. In their tent after lights out, Peter found himself listening to Tom's breathing. Once certain Tom was sound asleep, he would press his hand against the small of his back, holding it there until he himself fell asleep. On hot nights when they were shirtless, the heat radiating through Tom's skin mixed with the coolness of the beads of sweat was so thrilling that Peter barely slept at all.

Soon Peter was organizing his entire social calendar around opportunities for these late-night hand pressings, but he was extremely careful that it never became more than that. In high school their sleepovers lessened. Tom got a serious girlfriend, and Peter was the third wheel. He knew his place. It never occurred to him to tell. There were homosexuals in the West Village and the Castro marching for their right to do just that, but in the mid 1970s boys in Norwalk, Connecticut had no idea those people and those places even existed.

When they went to MIT together, everyone assumed they would be roommates. Peter was secretly grateful he had avoided that disaster. Still, as their friendship transcended from boyhood concerns into the first forays of adulthood, especially their passion for their respective fields of mathematics and applied physics, their bond only deepened. Whenever they were together they were enthralled with one another. Both had girlfriends. The two women would commiserate that they were the third wheel in Peter and Tom's relationship.

Dating came easy for both of them. In Peter's case, the girl was usually thrust upon him, facilitated by Tom. The male/female ratio on campus was four to one, but the common joke was that the ratio was practically even because out of every four men, two were undatable nerds, and one was a secret queer. Peter knew he was the latter. No one else suspected—except one of the girlfriends, and she never told. She treated him with a pitying kindness that Peter began to suspect was the best he ought to hope for.

One Friday night in their last year, the two couples were at the bar they frequented in Cambridge. Peter and Tom were celebrating having received job offers, which both arrived in the mail that week. Tom was going to California. Peter was staying in the Boston area. Graduation was two months away. The four of them sat in a booth, beer mugs and peanut shells between them, the two men seated together facing their dates, their usual arrangement. What was not usual was that after a fourth round, Tom put his hand on Peter's thigh, slipping over his crotch, searching the denim for his testicles. Peter was petrified.

They dropped their dates off at the sorority house and, without saying a word, walked to Tom's apartment. Once inside, the men made quick work of removing all their clothes. Peter had never been naked with another person in such a state, had never been kissed like Tom was kissing him. He did not quite know what to do, and he was shocked how Tom moved his body as though there was no mystery at all. It did not last long. The best part for Peter was that he got to spend the entire night with his arms wrapped around this man that he had loved for so long.

In the morning, Tom flashed Peter a sheepish grin, pulled on his sweats and announced he was going to the gym. When they met up that afternoon, it was as though their lovemaking had happened in a dream. Just as they came together, before even an awkward pause could commence, Tom launched into one of his dramatic stories. Frivolous, comical episodes were always happening to Tom, or at least this is how he preferred to cast his life to others. Peter wanted so badly to talk about the event, to have its reality co-signed, but Tom's swirling story yanked him back to their plutonic stance. For the rest of that day, and in the days after, they were merely best friends. It felt like a lie. But it was a lie that became increasingly comfortable. Each moment that came after it only compounded the lie's importance. The truth became a shadow that receded but never dissolved entirely. Somewhere within its outlines Peter guessed was his true self. Like a presence staring at you from the corner, you could forget it was there.

Two months passed, and they carried on as they always had. Tom was coy about exactly when he was leaving for California. In the hubbub of graduation and moving and goodbye parties, Peter lost track of him. It was a Sunday afternoon, after his family had left town and his friends had packed out and there was nothing to do, when Peter realized Tom was gone too. There was no need to go knock on his apartment door and be greeted by strangers. He could sense the absence. No goodbye.

Peter's heart had been broken at every stage of his friendship with Tom—since the night in the Scout tent when he first put his hand to the small of his back—but this was the only time he was brought to tears. He had understood the imperative not to talk about the event, but he had not consciously decided that he would never talk about it. In those two months he thought there would eventually be a still, quiet moment between them. Now the chance was lost. The next time they would see one another, they would be grown men in the eyes of the world, established in important jobs, and—who knows?—family men ensconced withing with dark green lawns and white picket fences. They would be living the kind of life where the illicit dalliances of youth cannot intrude. There had been brief moments in the past two months when he could have told Tom his true feelings, when he could have recast their entire secret life together, but these had been crossroads he had whistled past unaware that they might never come again. The moment wasn't right, he told himself. There would be more moments. Now, when Peter dared to gaze into his future, the road he found himself on was empty as far as eye could see, not a soul to greet him on either side. Peter wept for the life he could have had if only he'd had the courage to force the conversation, consequences be damned.

Years went by with no word exchanged between them. Peter heard through his mother, who had run into Mrs. Osberg at the salon, that Tom was still working at the aerospace company in California, making loads of money. Oh and was married with two kids. Good for him, Peter thought.

Then he got the call. The man gave his name as Bernard Gray, but it was his voice, though neutered of its former jocularity. He got to the point, feigning as though the first part of the conversation had already occurred. Said his employer had a job for him. Temporary, maybe two weeks, but with the possibility of a long-term pick up. Told him to fly to Los Angeles under the name Cameron Weis. This was his work name, how things were done.

Sensing the conversation was abrupt, Peter got out one question. "How can I reach you?"

"Just book the flight. I will know when you are there." Click.

Peter, who had been lonely a long time, interpreted Tom's secrecy only one way. Not only would they pick up where they left off, it just might mean the beginning of their life together.

Peter landed at LAX, walked outside, and somehow Tom was right there with his car. They shook hands. Peter said that Tom looked exactly the same, and joked about his own receding hairline that he concealed by keeping it buzzed tight.

They drove for some time, skirting around the populated sections of the city. Peter downloaded his entire life since graduation—careful to elide the very few details that would touch on his love life. Tom said very little, which was beginning to unnerve Peter, when they pulled into a lot before an enormous brick structure, some kind of abandoned plant. It was the middle of the afternoon.

Tom led him through an unlocked metal door into the empty, cavernous interior, and then into a rattletrap elevator, the kind with a hand-pulled accordion gate. He turned the key and they went down.

The basement was low and open, receding into a maze of hallways and smaller rooms, all flooded with red light. People milled about or stood gently rocking in the nooks—all men. Some wore business suits, others black leather biker gear, quite a few wore nothing at all. A large, hairy man in a jockstrap stood behind a bar serving alcohol. Somewhere through the walls speakers played thumping music.

Tom now took Peter by the hand and pulled him down one of the hallways. Soon they were in one of the small rooms. It was swept clean and empty except for a green metal desk that looked like it had been there since the Eisenhower era. Tom placed Peter on this desk and kissed him. A long, deep kiss that was just like their first kiss. He then carefully undid all of Peter's buttons and set his clothes aside. He stared at Peter's body for a long time, saying nothing.

They made love in the same fashion as the first time, a little rougher. They left as soon as they were finished.

The drive to Palmdale took an hour. Neither of them said a word until Tom dropped Peter off at his hotel. "Remember, you're Cameron, and you call me Bernard," Tom said. "Don't slip up."

Peter lay awake that night bewildered. His body had never felt so satisfied and whole, while his heart had never felt so uneasy. He had to remind himself that he was not stupid. Tom was still married, with a serious job. The man was not going to throw away his life over a long-dormant boyhood infatuation. This was by all appearances a fling. Still Peter was wracked with a thrilling hope that something might come of it. The biggest mistake of his life had been to let Tom make love to him without ever speaking of it again. That one non-decision had affected everything that happened to him after. Tomorrow, he vowed, he would not repeat it.

The next morning, Peter found himself in another elevator going down, though this one was all black glass and stainless steel, with a computerized voice that announced the destination. He and Tom exited into a long white-walled corridor, punctuated by a series of gray, windowless doors. Tom opened one and they were in a square conference room with three other men.

The man with the heavy mustache and broad smile stood up and offered his hand. "Cameron," he greeted. "Your reputation precedes you. You come highly recommended."

Peter reciprocated the handshake and the smile but was unsure what to say. Had they spoken with others in Boston? If so, why did he call him Cameron?

The man, who refrained from giving his own name, continued. "I can see that Bernard has told you exactly nothing about why we have brought you out here. I'm sure he's also spoken no more than seventeen words to you since the airport."

True on both counts. Peter was speechless.

"Around here we joke Cat's-got-his-tongue."

The other man at the table, unsmiling, said, "Cat's his wife's name."

The smiling man laughed. "Bernard manages some of our most sensitive proprietary interests. Please sit."

All of them wore dark suits with fat colorless neckties—except the old man sitting by himself in one of a row of chairs against the wall. He wore a trim, three-piece suit, robin's egg blue with brass buttons. It had to be from the early '60s, still pristine, smelling of mothballs and Old Spice. He sat rigidly, unmoving, like he was chained to the chair. His glistening gray eyes stared blankly through the younger men at the table.

The smiling man was talking vaguely about brick walls the project teams had run into and how he might help them get unstuck, but Peter was thinking about Tom's wife. He had not known her name. Cat, short for Catherine probably. He could picture her. All Tom's girlfriends at MIT looked the same. He forced himself to focus. He found himself asking, "Is it a problem in the math or in the physics?"

The smiling and the unsmiling man exchanged a look before the unsmiling man said, "We're not sure."

"That's bad," Peter said.

This made the old man snort with laughter. "That's bad," he repeated, chuckling. "He's got you there." He then wiped his nose with a handkerchief that was not his pocket square.

Peter was now intrigued enough to be distracted from his thoughts about Bernard/Tom. He placed his elbows on the table and leaned in.

The smiling man continued. "We've come into possession of a metal with unusual properties."

"Where did you find it?" Peter asked.

"We can't tell you that," said the unsmiling man.

"It's an alloy, mostly magnesium. But the magnesium isotope ratios are off normal from anything we see in nature."

"So it's manufactured. By whom?"

"We can't tell you that."

The smiling man shot an unsmiling look at the unsmiling man for the first time. He then returned his smile to Peter. "We actually don't know that it's manufactured. It may be the byproduct of an industrial process. Exhaust, if you will. We want to know if it is the product of some kind of propulsion system."

Peter thought of the parlor game where the participant reaches into a sealed box and has to describe the object within only by his fingertips, but he kept this joke to himself. He turned to the unsmiling man and asked, "Are you going to let me see it?"

He reached to the center of the table and nudged a small black object toward Peter. It was round with a depression in the center. The asymmetrical rim was wavy on one side with jagged teeth on the other. It looked like an ashtray that somebody's kid made in pottery class, which is why Peter had not noticed it. He picked it up to inspect. Heavy and smooth. No weld marks. The casting, if it had been cast, was unusual. The metal was deep black but when he put his eye right up to it, he could make out a fine marbled sheen like the hood of a Buick. He set it down, indicating he was ready to begin.

The unsmiling man explained the red-team/blue-team protocol. Bernard would lead the red team, studying the object according to a precise set of parameters. Cameron would lead the blue team, following the exact same parameters, and neither team would exchange any interaction or communication. At the end of the study, both teams would submit their work to a third group, with which there would also not be any interaction or communication. Cameron and Bernard were not to discuss their findings, or anything else about the project, ever.

Peter was so flummoxed by these instructions that he could not think of a fitting response except to make a joke. "You're not going to tell me this thing fell off of a Russian MIG? The Air Force loaned it out so you can put your best and brightest on it?"

"We can't tell you that," the unsmiling man repeated, adding, "But it does remind me. Have you or anyone you know ever been a member of the Communist Party?"

Peter very carefully said no, and decided never to joke with this guy again.

The smiling man called for a break and directed Bernard to show Cameron the coffee room.

After a quick tutorial, Peter learned how to work a Mr. Coffee machine so large it was built into the wall. As the nozzle dispensed the steaming black liquid into a styrofoam cup, Peter made his move. It was not the most ideal setting, but they were alone and he was not sure how much longer that would be the case.

"It's hard to believe, the two of us together again."

"Not for long," Tom said, handing him the cup. "Red team/blue team, remember?"

"Do you think we can make this work, you and me?"

"I doubt it. The old guy in there has been working on this since '65."

"I'm not talking about the ashtray. I'm talking about us."

Tom stared at the buttons on the face of the machine. "He was at Los Alamos. You should ask him about it."

Just as before, Peter felt himself being pushed back into secrecy. But this time it was not with a funny story and devilish grin. It was a darker, much stronger force. He chose to ignore it.

Tom plucked his own styrofoam cup out of the machine and headed for the door. Peter went after him.

"You're really not going to say anything more?"

"I think you'll find that the compartmentalization policies here are more extreme than other jobs you have worked. It'll take some getting used to."

"Don't you think about what we could have, what it might be like?"

Tom reached for the door. "It's best not to think long term with work like this. Just keep your head down, do the math." Then he flashed his old grin that Peter remembered so warmly. "And enjoy the weather while you're here, man."

Peter grabbed Tom's forearm, dropping his voice to a whisper so not to be misunderstood. "How are we ever supposed to get anywhere?"

Tom let the smile linger, and put a flinty glimmer in his eye so that he would not be misunderstood. "We're not."

Peter went back into the conference room, failing to notice that Tom did not follow. He approached the old man in the blue suit. "I hear you were at Los Alamos. Must have been something."

The old man chuckled. "Happiest years of my life, up there working on the bomb." Then he waved Peter toward him with a curl of his fingers, like he wanted to confide something. Peter stooped slightly.

"After the drop, we caused no end of trouble. Not like that anymore. These boys run a much tighter ship." He patted Peter on the shoulder and nudged him toward the others.

There were more men around the table now, all of them with the same disposition of the unsmiling man. Peter pegged them as lawyers. The paperwork they presented took the rest of the morning, and it scared the hell out of him. He read more of the Espionage Act of 1917 and the National Security Act of 1947, particularly the sections pertaining to treason, than he would have thought necessary for a two-week contacting gig to solve a math problem. Prison terms at Leavenworth were stipulated, at which point the unsmiling man made a joke about how the electric chair at Leavenworth had been replaced with the much more humane lethal injection chamber. Even though it was made perfectly clear to Peter that he shall not discuss his work here with anyone, it was all made to feel banal and perfunctory. The lawyers acted just like bored financiers in a car dealership, nudging him along through the paperwork with assurances that everyone's got to do it before the fun can begin. Peter figured that there was no need for them to give him the drill sergeant routine while they were methodically binding him to his chair with red tape.

Peter noticed something else in the stacks of legal documents neatly sorted across the entire surface of the conference table. He was a passable accountant and always liked to know where his paycheck was coming from, especially when he took government jobs. In the string of contract gigs he had done for NASA and offices within the Pentagon, Peter had never seen anything like this arrangement. His direct employer for this job was financing through a subcontract to a small outfit called Quartz Associates that held a standard defense service contract with the Defense Department, an arrangement that made no sense for the sprawling, expensive facility he'd walked into that morning, or the sensitive work they were asking him to do. Peter realized he was about to go to work for a shell company that was being funneled god knows how much taxpayer dollars, all without the knowledge of those taxpayers or their representatives in Congress who signed over the money in the first place. Peter was being asked to join a criminal enterprise. The job did not even seem that interesting.

If not for the prospect of being close to Tom, he might have considered walking away.

When it was over, all the documents signed, Peter looked at these men and asked, "What are you all doing down here?"

"You don't need to worry about that," the smiling man said, unsmiling now. He pointed to the ashtray. "Your only job is to figure out what that thing is made out of."

Peter was in a daze as he stepped into the hallway. Tom was there, pushing a fresh cup of coffee and a key card into his hands. He pointed to a gray door with an electronic lock at the far end of the corridor. That was to be his workspace.

"Can we get lunch?" Peter wanted to get Tom alone again, this time to learn what kind of job he had just signed up for.

Tom pointed again at the door. "They will take care of all your needs. You get your own girl. She can get you literally anything. Just ask. They're great here with that sort of thing."

Tom turned and walked in the opposite direction, toward his own door at the other end of the corridor.

Peter called after him. "When will I see you?"

Without turning Tom replied, "You won't."

Peter walked backwards, keeping Tom in sight until he slipped through the door and was gone. He was alone for only a moment. Once he passed through his own door, he met his secretary who took his coat and lunch order. Peter worked in this room for a lot longer than two weeks. He never saw Tom again.

Carver Section, Washington, D.C. – 1964

The black Lincoln Continental was parked at the corner of Maryland Avenue and H Street, the great bone-white bell jar of the Capitol Building looming in the rear window. Two men in black suits, one carrying a brown paper sack under his arm, got in the front. The long car rumbled to life and rolled around the corner, slowly turning through a maze of narrow streets and terraces. It stopped at the top of a dead-end street flanked on both sides by one story row houses.

A third man sat in the middle seat in the back of the car so that he had an unobstructed view straight ahead through the windshield. He leaned back against the bench, legs spread, hands resting on his thighs, relaxed. It was a comfortable car, and he knew how to get comfortable in it. He spent a lot of time right where he was.

He wore the same black suit and skinny black tie as the other two. It was their uniform. He was comfortable in that too, as he had been in uniforms his entire adult life. When he was sixteen, it was a dark blue Pullman coat. Then the Army. Now this. He was not sure it was an upgrade, though the pay certainly was. Like those jobs, this one mostly consisted of waiting around for other people. The new partners were usually gone for hours. They took their sweet time to do anything, especially lunch. He did not nap, though he could stretch out head to toe on the back bench, nor he did read. He just sat and stared through the windshield, watched the people walk by wherever the car happened to be parked, and thought about all he would do with the money in his next paycheck.

This third man's name was Ronald. The partners called him Ronny, which was a name only his mother used. Of course they could call him whatever they wanted. He was not comfortable with that, but there was no choice but to get used to it.

The partners were yacking as soon as they were in the car. Part of the reason they took so long to do anything was that they never shut up. The one with the paper bag dumped its contents on the seat between them and began sorting. Ronald could not see what it all was except what the partners picked up.

"Look what I found at the gag shop," the passenger-side partner said, holding up a dashboard bauble. He licked the suction cup and slapped it onto the center of the vinyl panel, then gave it a little flick, causing the hula skirt to swish back and forth. He looked sideways to Ronald. "Funny, aye?" Ronald nodded.

Then he turned to the driver-side partner, showing him a red wire that he began snaking down his shirt collar. "I got a new look for this one. You're going to love it."

"You really think so," the other said indifferently as he opened a clam-shell makeup kit and placed it on the dashboard. He finished the story he had been telling about his wife's overpriced underwear getting chewed up by their new, overpriced washing machine, while he used the applicator to gently smear white powder around his eyes.

The other unbuckled his pants and snaked the red wire down his leg while he tried to tell a joke about how the same thing happened to Marilyn Monroe's knickers, but he could not quite remember how to get to the punchline. He abruptly switched subjects. "Tell me again why we have to do the clown act? I don't understand it."

"You still sleeping through the briefings? Of course you are. The interview has to scare 'em a little. And the icing on the cake is that all the weird little details make it so that if they ever tell anyone about us, people will think they're nuts. The shrinks have this all figured out."

"Shows how much they know. Who says clowns are scary?"

"Oh clowns are scary."

"Who you kidding? Happy clowns with the big nose and the balloons at the kids' birthday parties? You like clowns, Ronny Boy?"

"I like them fine," Ronald replied.

"If you're so smart, explain to me why clowns are scary."

"Because," he said slowly while blending the white powder into his skin tone around the temples, "clowns got their own rules and nobody knows what they are. They could do anything." He pushed his forehead up to the rearview mirror and brought the rim of his black fedora down to the white edge. "We got to make these people think we might reach out and break their necks"—his hand jabbed into the other man's face and snapped sharply—"but without using any of the mafia words, and without making any sudden movements." Then he let out his best Vincent Price laugh—a rolling, scratchy cackle from the back of his throat.

"That's real good. You should use that at parties. The way you do your voice, sounds just like him." As he bent over to pull the wire through a hole in the ankle of his left sock, he added, "If it works, it works,"

"It works like a charm."

It did not work on everyone, Ronald thought to himself, which was the reason he was in the car.

Once he was done pulling the last of the wire out his jacket sleeve, he lifted up a half-circle plastic brace with two thick, round prongs on each end.

"What is that?"

"It's the neck thingies on Frankenstein. I got it at the gag shop."

"No."

"I can make it work," he said, pressing the brace beneath his collar so that only the prongs were visible.

"I told you how my wife likes expensive clothes. Coco Chanel. I learned something from my wife that is directly applicable to our job, believe it or not. Before you leave the house, ladies, check yourself in the mirror and take off the last accessory you put on." He pointed at the man's neck, who did as he was told.

"How come you get to be Vincent Price but I can't be a Frankenstein robot?"

"It's corny."

Suddenly angry, "Why you got to say that particular thing? That's going to be in my head now, mess with the performance."

"It's corny."

"You know I'm from Oklahoma. Those are fighting words."

"Please, look at you. You couldn't fight your way out of a sack of manure."

The partners spilled out of the car, shushing each other as they walked down the sidewalk.

Ronald's gaze came to rest on the dashboard bauble. He did not in fact find it funny, though it was ridiculous. It was a Sambo figurine, the shape and size of a pear, sausage arms out in imitation of the hula dance, the whole lump black as coal except for the grass skirt, bright red lips, and two white dots for eyes. He'd seen this image his whole life, though never this particularly absurd juxtaposition with the Hula Girl. White people seemed to always have them around—sitting on their shelves, in their yards, peeking out from picture frames or their newspapers, now in their cars. They were like a talisman to ward away... what exactly? He realized that he'd never really thought much about them. Perhaps, Ronald thought, the job was getting to him. The waiting and the interviews were making him contemplative. More and more, the job was making him wonder what was in the back of things.

For one, there were different versions to create different effects. The pear-shaped character was usually exceedingly polite and even more stupid. Other times they were randy, usually lusting for a white woman. An entirely different version was ape-like and violent. The whole point, it seemed to Ronald, was to remind white people that the proper reaction when encountering a black person was either to laugh, scream, or kill, but mostly to laugh.

These little lumps of plastic, and plaster, and sometimes actual polished coal had marked the crossroads of his life as surely as if they'd been planted there to direct his fate, and that of every other person who bore his skin tone. How could such an absurdity have this much power? How could such an insane idea get its start? Had a committee of white people, some time after slave days, gotten together and hatched this strategy? Had they fashioned the first Sambo doll and placed orders with toy makers across the country? And then paid the shipping postage to have them sent to every white housewife in the land? The things were so ubiquitous and so effective in their purpose that it was hard not to think it was planned. But no, Ronald had been in enough committee rooms—those run by white men who thought themselves masters of the universe, and those run by black men whose lives depended on their being twice as effective—to know the pronouncements made in such rooms implode upon impact with the real world. The truth was more organic than that. The figures were a mirror reflection of how white people preferred to think of themselves—their guile, wisdom, and bravery, their poised, civilized decorum. The figures gave them permission not to have to think about him—Ronald—as a person inhabiting the same plane of existence with them. He was fine to have around, even useful some days—days like today, he suspected—but as a fellow human being, no, he was as impossible to take seriously as the little men in the flying saucers.

"Mother fucking nigger."

The partners were back in the car quicker than their usual interview.

"That did not work."

"Fucking niggers." He was red-faced and shaking.

"He made fun of your Vincent Price."

"And I should have—I wish I'd—cut his nuts off right then." Spit flew from his lips onto the windshield. His partner made him drink from a canteen of water, and he alternated between gulps of air and water. Then he flung the canteen to the floor, gripped the steering wheel like he was wringing a neck, and he said no more.

"Ronny Boy, batter up." The partner recited the details from the briefing. "Steffon Jones. Seventy-one years old. Works as a janitor for the, uh, doesn't matter. Keeps the items in a Jim Dandy-brand potato sack under the floorboards of the porch. There is a second item, a wheel with a depression in the center, that he may keep in a separate location. There are two pickaninnies in the backyard. Keep them out of it. No interview. Just make the exchange and get back to the car."

Ronald grabbed the satchel and was out of the car before the other one had a chance to catch his breath and suggest another course.

Steffon Jones stood waiting behind his screen door when the third man in a black suit came to his stoop. Unlike the first two, this one kept to the sidewalk. He set a heavy black satchel on the porch against the post.

"That's a nice bag," Jones said.

Ronald looked at it. "It is."

"I can't do anything with a bag like that."

"That may be, but it's what's in it that ought to be of use to you, Mr. Jones."

"Yes, sir."

He stepped outside, aided by a cane. At the end of the porch he lowered himself to one knee and pulled up a plank. It took some time for him to fish out the sack, right himself on his feet again, and shuffle back to his visitor. Ronald reached up the steps and took the sack, peering inside. The stuff looked no different than slag shards and bits of charcoal. No wheel. He pretended to inspect the contents while he thought of an excuse to engage further. He was told not to interview but he didn't see he had a choice. The partners had not gotten this far, and even their money was not going to seal the deal. The Sambo figurine meant they could bully, threaten, and murder whenever and wherever they pleased, but the tradeoff was that they could never set foot onto a man's porch and have a simple conversation. This was of course the reason Ronald was in the car in the first place.

"Mr. Jones, do you mind if I sit? You put my partners in a state, and I'm hoping they collect themselves before I return."

"No, sir. Suit yourself."

Ronald sat in the second of two wooden chairs. A small round table like a lamp would sit on in a living room corner stood between them. He set the sack on the floor and made himself look at ease.

"That was brave of you."

Jones eyed him, mulling whether to take the bait. "No, sir. You learn to take your measure of what a man is capable of. I wagered that if they were going to kill me, they would not have come up in here dressed like a pair of damn clowns."

"But they desperately need these items."

"Do they now?" Jones asked, as if that was news to him. "Well, I left part of this food in the Argonne Forest, so if agents of the United States government are willing to kill me over a bag of rocks, they can keep it."

"Who says we work for the government?"

Jones chuckled without cracking a smile. He lowered himself into the opposite chair. Ronald produced a pack of Lucky Strikes, offering one to Jones. They smoked in silence.

Ronald finally asked, "What do you think these things actually are?" Planting seeds of doubt was a required part of the interview process, but he genuinely wanted to know the old man's opinion. For his part, Ronald had no idea, only that the men who hired him took it very seriously. Whenever they picked these items up, the partners would deliver them by car to the Air Force Systems Command at Andrews Air Force Base in Maryland. Ronald was not invited on those drives, thank God. He got to go home, stash the suit in the closet, and put the whole business out of mind.

"I know what they are," Jones said, "and they are not of this world."

"Isn't it more likely they are some sort of secret military aircraft that we don't want the Russians to know about?"

"That's just what I used to think. I don't know if they told you this, or if they even know it, but I've seen them before."

Ronald betrayed no expression.

"I worked in the Capitol Building in the summer of '52. My job was to take out the trash from the senators' offices and conference rooms, clean out the ashtrays and spittoons, replenish the cigars, make everything real nice for when the senators returned. That's what I was doing when one of the fellers called me to the window. We saw seven bright white discs, and an eighth that was fiery orange. They were floating motionless almost directly above the dome. We watched them for maybe two minutes until they moved southwest over the airport. There they disappeared, just vanished."

Ronald had never heard about this incident, but he'd heard so many others just like it that he implicitly believed the story. "Did you call anyone?"

"Of course not. They already think we're deranged."

"What did you do?"

"I finished wiping down the spittoons and went home. It happened again one week later. Luckily I didn't see anything, but I heard about it the next day. And we all thought they were Russian bombers, or more likely our own. Some big Air Force general gave a press conference and blamed it all on the weather. The rest of us did not think about it anymore."

He leaned over the little table, pointing with this cigarette. "I'll tell you this, sir. It's one thing to see lights in the sky and call them clouds. When you see them up close, like I did last week, there's no doubt about what they are."

Ronald knew he did not have much more time. He did not want to risk the partners returning. So here he picked up Mr. Jones's story. "Tuesday, 10:17pm, you are on your porch smoking a cigarette before bed. You don't smoke in the house as a rule because your grandson suffers from asthma. You are startled by a bright light that suddenly appears over your house. You get onto the sidewalk and look up to see a doughnut shaped object the length of a school bus. It is made of metal, but the center is pure light. A blinding white light. The object begins to wobble. There is a grinding sound like rusty metal gears locking up. You hear something pelting your roof and backyard, like hail. Then a second doughnut of the same dimensions descends. It holds the first doughnut in a beam of light, which seems to stabilize it, and they shoot straight up together, gone in the blink of an eye."

Jones was impressed. "And how is it you know that story that I only told to one person in the backroom of the bar down the street, if you don't work for the government?"

"Not only did you tell your friend, Mr. Stapleton, that story, you showed him a wheel with a depression in the center."

A twinkle and a grin brightened the elder's face for the first time.

"I'm going to need that piece as well, Mr. Jones."

"Like I said, you can keep it."

"But where is it?"

Jones let go of all pretension. A belly laugh rolled out of him. "Your hand is resting on it, son."

Ronald jerked back. His wrist had been resting on the smooth edge of what he had assumed was an ashtray with prongs on one side perfectly spaced to support a cigarette. He flicked his own nub into the street, placed the wheel in the sack and stepped off the porch. He should have kept walking, and in the months and years ahead he would come to regret that he had not. But he was overcome with an urge to do a kindness for Mr. Jones. He picked up the satchel, which was quite heavy, and placed it inside the door. While in the transom he saw down the central hallway into the backlot, where a boy and girl were playing four square with a large red ball. He let the screen door snap shut, but lingered on the stoop.

"It's none of my business, sir, but what will you do with it?" Jones had not moved from the chair. "Buy a better future. Send my two grandchildren to college. Their daddy's in Vietnam, and their mother... well, I don't expect her back. You probably knew about that already."

"No. It didn't make it into the briefing book."

"My advice, son. Get out from this while you can. This is white man's mess. We've got bigger fish, anyhow."

Ronald walked back to the car turning over Mr. Jones's parting words in his mind. He'd never considered leaving his job, but now that he was considering it, he had no idea how he might go about it. What would he tell the partners? More to the point, what would they do? Let him go be a bank clerk or a school teacher knowing, as he did, why they put on clown makeup and knocked on random citizens' doors? It was moot. Besides, Ronald was holding out for his own bag of money, or the equivalent in a government pension. He wanted a comfortable life. The partners might not offer him that. Mr. Jones's counsel was no bed of roses either.

The least he could do was commit the street address to memory in case he ever wanted to come this way again. It would be real nice, he thought, in thirty or forty years, to learn what dividends Uncle Sam's bag of money had accrued to the Jones family.

Muroc Airfield, Pancho's Bar – 1948

A crystalline blue sky, clear as plateglass and redolent with the light beaming up from the white desert floor, throbbed above the remote military outpost. There was no wind, no movement, no sound, and yet the blue light was so intense that it seemed to quake. This was the kind of sky the test pilots lived for, why they were all living out in this desolation. Today none of their airplanes or rocket-propelled aircraft ripped the sky, and none of their explosions peeled across the desert. It was Friday afternoon, the day before V-E Day, and the whole base was on leave for the holiday.

At Pancho's, all the windows and doors into the barroom were flung open to let the spring air and the light brighten the dark, dusty timbers of the interior. The bar was already crowded, though not half as full as it would be in a few hours.

Saul Travers came up the porch steps and entered through the front door, a man at ease with his conspicuousness. He was taller than most and stocky, having recovered the body weight he'd lost since the war. His gait was a rolling wobble from where the surgeons reattached his left leg two inches shorter than it was before. The pate of his forehead had a bulge and a deep crease where they put the metal plate. His left eye was made of glass, painted to look just like the right eye, but lifeless. He had let his black, frizzy hair grow long, and it had turned white over the plate. Walking into bars was not something Saul enjoyed doing anymore. His conspicuousness was compounded by the fact that he had arrived at Muroc that morning. No one here knew him, except for the one who had told him to come sit at Pancho's Bar and wait.

A few patrons turned to face him as he hobbled past, their gazes locking with recognition on one or more points of deformity, and then sliding on into oblivion. It was an elision that came naturally to veterans toward their fellow wounded brethren, albeit with frequent opportunities to practice, a non-gesture made as much out of respect as discomfort. And just like that, Saul was invisible again, a curious effect of his many injuries that had its uses in the kind of work Saul was tasked with.

But one man seated at the end of the bar knew Saul and called out to him immediately. Frank Amato dropped his hand on Saul's shoulder and pulled him over, all smiles and backslapping. He was genuinely thrilled to see him, more cheerful than Saul remembered, not at all drunk. Pancho, he said, had taught her barkeeps to make a gimlet with jalapenos that was just delicious. Soon he had two in hand and guided Saul to a table by a window that looked out onto the crisscrossing airstrips embedded into the sun-blasted lakebed. The efficiency with which Frank was able to sweep him into the corner away from the others made Saul wonder if Frank was the man he was supposed to meet here. He dismissed this notion as soon as it occurred to him. Frank would never put himself in that position.

During the war both men had been recruited into a select group within the Military Intelligence Service whose job it was to collect and intercept signals intelligence. Back then Saul had been fearless and self-assured, even a little reckless in the face of danger—all traits, paired with his intellect, that got him recruited in the first place. This made his maiming all the more tragic, and Frank was curious to take his measure of the man in his current diminished state.

The two wartime friends raised their cocktail glasses and chinked the rims in a toast to V-E Day. The jalapenos bit into Saul's sensitive pallet, and masked the stiffness of the drink. He set it aside.

"What brings you to Muroc?" Frank boomed, as if his arrival was the best thing to have happened here all week.

"I didn't know you were here either," Saul replied.

"Going on a year now," Frank explained. "The chiefs at Wright Field needed someone to keep tabs on these corn-fed, hot head pilots out here at the ends of the Earth, so naturally they sent an Italian from the Bronx." Big laugh, followed by a big slurp of the fire water. "How's the family?"

Both Frank and Saul had three children. During his incapacitation, Saul's wife Adina had resettled their family in Dayton, and secured for

Saul a rather mundane desk job with the Advanced Technical Intelligence Center where he could work during his recuperation. Once the Army realized that the mind under the tantalum plate was intact, they were eager to maintain their asset, for Saul was a gifted analyst and linguist. For two years he'd stayed out of sight behind the desk, that is until recent developments put him back in the field. Saul declined to reveal any of this to Frank, but he offered up that his youngest was going into first grade in the fall. Frank's wife Mary and their three boys lived on the base with him. Saul had heard that Mary had recently given birth to a fourth child, a daughter, who died before she left the hospital. Naturally, this went unmentioned.

Saul was careful not to let his eyes scan the barroom to see if anyone might be taking particular interest in him. He was also careful not to seem uninterested in his drink, and so took occasional sips. He desperately needed for this conversation not to be happening right now, but there was nothing to be done except to get to the end of it.

"This takes me back to the last time we saw one another," Saul said, feigning reminiscence. "We'd gotten our assignments and lost track of one another, which can't be avoided, I suppose, under the circumstances. What camp were you sent to?"

Frank's loose smile evaporated. "Ehh, I was in a few of them. All the Pollock names run together."

"It was Dachau for me."

The two men merely stared at one another. Dachau. Poland. There was nothing to say about these words, and nothing was what was usually said about them. Still, Saul pressed on.

"There's something I've wondered about, about those of us who went in first. Did you ever talk about it?"

"We filed our report. We were debriefed."

"Did you ever tell Mary what you saw there?"

Frank could not understand where this was coming from. "God no. What's gotten into you?" Since Frank did not want to know the answer to his own question, and was eager to get off this morbid topic, he pointed Saul's attention to a man who just walked into the bar leading a pack of other pilots.

"See that man there? He broke the sound barrier. Went supersonic."

Saul was shocked. "When?"

"Last October. He's done it a bunch more since then. They've cracked the code."

"My God…" Saul was awestruck by this revelation. Aircraft design was nowhere near his area of expertise, though recent developments had sent him into the books on this topic. He knew enough to know it was a shattering technical accomplishment. "This would be the biggest story since Moses parted the Red Sea, and we've been sitting on it for six months? The propaganda value alone."

"You know Wright Field, it's secrets all the way down."

"Who is he?"

"Just some hick from West Virginia. If you'd hear him talk you wouldn't think he could put two and two together. But he's smart. They're all smart. Too smart in ways. I think the chiefs wish we could put monkeys in these jets." Frank then tapped his shoulder, and motioned for them both to hunch forward across the table. "Speaking of secrets, I hear you were part of the Aztec crash recovery. Good on you, getting out from behind that desk they've chained you to in Dayton." He clinked Saul's glass on the tabletop and drank.

Now Saul knew that Frank was probing, that he was finally getting to the point of this exercise. He was less sure if he was being entrapped, though that was now a live possibility. In any case, he could not answer Frank's question, and Frank knew that if he really knew about Aztec.

"I don't know what you mean," Saul answered, pretending to sip from his glass. "Office life suits me fine."

"Was it really as big as they say? I heard from an OSS guy, they had to cut it in half just to get it off the mesa. Took two weeks to clean up."

Saul turned his gaze to the window, through a stand of cotton-woods and beyond them at the Joshua trees still as mummies twisting out of the desert floor. He knew that Frank was not repeating mere gossip, because no one with actual knowledge of Aztec would have let those two details become gossip. Frank was reciting the lines he'd been given. Saul was caught, and all there was to do was wait out the clock. This day was not going to end as he hoped it would when he left his house before dawn that morning, when he kissed his sleeping children in their beds. He had such mad hopes. Now he doubted he would ever set foot in that house again, though he refused to let that dark fate cloud his judgment in these final crucial minutes.

"Dachau," he repeated. "I told Adina about it. The stacks of bodies. That terrible smell of death and lye, of dead flesh on living bodies. The ash heaps. The survivors were so thin and white they weren't re-ally human anymore. She just stared at me as though I wasn't saying anything at all. And then she put a kettle on, and made me drink some tea. Frank, you were there. Shouldn't we tell everyone? Shouldn't we teach our children these things?"

Frank was so affronted by this that he seemed to forget his mis-sion. His voice now became much quieter than when he was spilling state secrets, and ringing with anger. "Of course not. Never. They're not going to understand. I don't want them to understand. It was a terrible thing, but it's done now. We won, remember?"

He lifted his drink but stopped to say, "Tell my children? Have you lost your mind? It's my duty as a husband and a father, as a man, to protect them. We have to be men now."

"We keep so much from them. It's like we don't trust anyone, even ourselves. Why is that?"

Frank shook his head, letting the disgust he'd been carefully stanching flood out of him. "I think your injury has gotten to you. I think the field doc screwed on that metal plate too tight. You going to tell your children that story? Gather around the fire kiddies and let Pops tell you about the time when everything flashed white and I woke up a half-blind cripple. Are you ever going to tell them that?"

With a nod of his head, Saul conceded the point. Frank repeated himself, "We have to be men."

Their faces were close, nearly nose to nose. Saul's face craned at an angle so his one good eye could focus. Frank glared into that one eye.

"What happened on the mesa, Saul?"

"I told you."

"You didn't. You can talk to me. I've been cleared."

"No one is cleared for what I know."

"What did you see?"

The thin crust of decorum snapped within him and an ice shelf of silence collapsed. It had only been, what, six weeks—a lifetime—and he'd not said a word. Oh yes he'd filed reports and sat for the debriefs but he'd never formulated the words that described what he truly believed. It was a pristine job, executed flawlessly. The clean-up was complete in two weeks, and even before then he began plotting this job, the one that brought him to Pancho's. All he had wanted to do was tell someone, and Frank was the last chance he would ever get.

"I saw their bodies! I saw a living being from another world!"

Frank leaned back in his chair. He had not expected that answer, but he was also convinced that he was not speaking with a sane man. His smile returned. "No you didn't, Saul. Sure, they were mangled. It was a crash."

"It did not look like a crash. None of it makes any sense."

"It was one of ours. These saucers, they are ours. We've had them at Muroc. Last July, six silvery discs zipped overhead, caused a big stir. Over the premier test range for experimental aircraft. Makes sense to me."

"It's not supposed to make sense. That's the whole point," Saul gasped. He was desperate to share the awareness he'd gained. "Just last month, three scientists at White Sands tracked a disc with a theodolite for thirty seconds. It made steep climbs and erratic maneuvers that were impossible for any pilot to survive. They clocked it at 18,000 miles per hour. The saucers are not ours."

Just then a green Army car turned and rumbled up the gravel road to Pancho's. Both men watched it through the open window.

"They just want to have a little conversation," Frank said.

"We both know that's not so."

Saul stood out of his chair and hobbled around the end of the table. He reached into his inside coat pocket and pulled out a large yellow envelope that contained six enlarged photographs and their negatives. Frank was not the intended recipient but he would have to do. He put the envelope in Frank's hand, pleading, "You should at least look at these before you turn them in."

Frank shoved the envelope into his own coat pocket. His job was done, and he wanted nothing more than to turn to the window, finish his drink, and be glad he never had to look on this particular mark ever again. But he was curious. He eyed Saul's face, the smooth half that resembled the man he once knew. The old Saul would have clocked him, just for the hell of it, and been out the back door in a flash. He would have put up a chase, and he would have made it pretty far. He had the fight in him that was nowhere apparent in the pitiful, broken man tottering before him now. Saul's one eye, wide and despairing like a beggar, bore into him as he made his last appeal.

"You have some sway. Use it. The earth is being visited by a race of beings who can cross the stars. They figured out how to do it and not destroy themselves. No war. No more camps. An unimaginable future. It could all start right here, right now. All we have to do is tell people."

Frank simply stared at him, the same blank stare Saul had received from his wife, his doctors, his old friends, any civilian he'd tried to convey some experience from the war. It was as though he had said nothing at all.

Frank turned sideways in his chair to make sure Saul made it out the front door, the transit of which would make him somebody else's problem. His only thought as he watched the cantering, slumped back was that he'd never seen anyone so unmanned as Saul Travers.

Once outside Saul climbed into the car without a word. As the driver pulled around the circular driveway Saul watched with a reflexive giggle as Frank lunged down the porch steps, buckled over and spewed the jalapeno gimlet and the rest of the contents of his stomach all over the alfalfa bushes. He had looked at the pictures.

The Mesa

Solon Brown pulled out of his driveway just as the sun was coming up over the peaks, another long day ahead of him. He was to drive 80 miles from his home in Aztec, New Mexico to Cortez, Colorado, where he had a meeting with church leaders of that town. Then he would backtrack 20 miles to his own church, Mancos Baptist, where he would spend most of the day preparing for the Sunday service. Then 220 miles to the Hopi Reservation in Arizona where he taught adult English classes. Then, after crossing every axis of the Four Corners, back home, not in time for dinner but in time to kiss his children goodnight. None of this was to be.

A few miles northeast of Aztec, where Route 550 crossed Hart Canyon Road, his eye was drawn to a patchwork of brush fires flickering on the top of a mesa. Several vehicles were parked on the edge of the mesa and more were driving on the dirt road that led to it. A pickup truck was pulled off at the intersection. A man he knew from town, who worked in the oil fields, sat in the bed. Solon pulled over and rolled down his passenger-side window.

"They say some kind of plane went down, and that there's dead airmen," the man said. "I ain't going near it. They could use a preacher though."

Solon did not make a conscious choice whether to keep on 550 to Cortez or turn onto the dirt road to the mesa. He did not have a conscious thought of any kind but to follow his calling. He would never drive past this crossroads again without being reminded of this fateful nonchoice.

The service roads in this section of New Mexico were laid down by the El Paso Oil Company, which maintained a series of drip tanks nearby. The mesa was five miles from the turn off, and in a few minutes Solon parked his car with the others. He scrambled up a soft sandstone embankment, reciting the Psalm of David aloud to calm his nerves and prepare his soul for whatever awaited him beyond the rim.

The aircraft was not like any he had ever seen or heard of. It was enormous, at least 100 feet in diameter. Round. A domed center that tapered to thin edges. Dull gray metal, perfectly smooth with no apparent damage. It sat on the rock where it had come down and was tipped at a 12-degree angle. Several stands of juniper trees on the one side of the plateau had broken branches or were snapped in two, some of them still aflame. There was no sound. No smell but woodsmoke.

Solon thought that he ought to have been wracked with fear by this eerie sight. Had he been alone he would have turned back and left whatever this was to the proper authorities, whomever that might be. But there were people everywhere, people he knew and others he did not. Some were his neighbors. Mr. and Mrs. Knight, two local ranchers, were keeping a watchful distance. Bill Ferguson and Doug Noland from the oil company were darting about taking pictures. Two police officers paced from one group to the next doling out half-hearted commands that seemed to have no effect. One of these was Manuel Sandoval, a friendly patrolman whom Solon would sometimes run into at gas stations and diners during his long drives. Half a dozen others, oil workers from the looks of their clothes, were walking all over the topside of the craft. They crisscrossed its surface, stepping gingerly, occasionally tapping the metal with their steel-toed boots. The metal made no sound when they did this.

Bill and Doug rushed to Solon as soon as they noticed him. Bill looked grave and determined, clutching a Kodak 35mm rangefinder camera slung around his neck. Doug, who was nineteen, could barely contain his excitement. He brandished a firepole and took lunging steps rather than walk, unconsciously pantomiming the action panels of Buck Rogers comics he'd consumed as a boy. They offered to take Solon to the bodies, if he was willing. As they walked around the rim of the craft, the two oil men explained the sequence of events up to that point.

The craft came down well before dawn. Officer Sandoval was finishing up his night patrol shift when he saw the thing wobbling through the air. He followed it here. The first people on the mesa were the oil workers who were worried the brush fires might spread to the drip tanks. It was still dark, and the great disc was shrouded in smoke, dappled with bright undulating shimmers. As Bill came up the embankment he thought that each point of light was a separate chunk of burning wreckage. When he realized that the lights were reflections from the fires, that the craft was one immense slab, he became overwhelmed by the most intense curiosity he had ever felt in his life. From the company truck he grabbed the camera and the firepole, and he and Doug set about their investigation.

Most of the pictures he took were of a Sikorsky H-5 helicopter, though he did not know that's what it was called. It arrived just as the sun was coming up, circled the mesa many times and flew away. None of the oil men had ever seen a helicopter before. Bill assumed it had come from wherever the disc had come from, that they were part of the same squadron. Doug called it a giant mechanical dragonfly.

The more they studied the disc the stranger it seemed. It looked to be made of aluminum, but it wasn't aluminum. There were no seams, no weld marks, no rivets. No propellers or jet intake or moving parts of any kind. They were tapping its surface with the firepole, which somehow caused the door to open. This is where they brought the preacher.

Solon stood in the entrance to a narrow corridor, careful to keep his feet steadied on the sandy ground, careful not to touch the metal.

There were two bodies face down on the floor. The limbs and torsos were small, the heads largish. They looked like children. They wore tight fitting coveralls. The skin on their hands and heads was charred dark brown.

Solon knelt and prayed the same prayers that he had offered up by the bedsides of the deceased countless times.

This requiem was interrupted by the shouts of the two police officers. The cavalry was coming, they said. With the sun high overhead, bathing the craft and the surrounding desert in light that cast no shadows, the fifteen residents from the Four Corners gathered on the edge of the mesa. They watched a caravan of military trucks barrel full speed along the rocky access road.

Saul Travers was seated on a bench in the back of the lead truck, dispensing orders to the field commanders. The first priority, before they went near the craft, was to collect and neutralize information. The soldiers would form pairs and interview each civilian in isolation. First, ask them why they are here, who told them to come, and to list everything they did from their decision to come up to the present moment. Then make sure they understand the following. This event is extremely important to the United States of America. As citizens they are responsible for our national security. They are not to tell anyone about what happened here, not even their wives, their pastor, or closest relations. They must always act as though the event never happened. Sharing any details about what they saw here will put their lives and the lives of their family in mortal danger. Saul added, if anyone resists or goes near the craft, shoot them.

There were no questions. Everyone in the truck understood what needed to be done. Whether they understood the reasons behind it was not important to them. Only that morning had Saul been briefed on the full picture, which had too many holes for his comfort. His briefers tried to assure him that it was not for classification rules that they seemed coy. They genuinely did not know what these objects were or where they came from. But it was not the first time something like this had happened.

Eight months earlier, an unknown craft had crashed under similar circumstances in a different section of New Mexico. The Army base in the area had thoroughly botched the response. For reasons surpassing all understanding, they put out a press release stating that the Army had captured a flying disc. This was printed in newspapers across the country before the retraction caught up with it. The wreckage lay strewn across a rancher's fields for a week. Half the town knew all about it. The rancher was about to go on a radio program and tell the whole story. Only at the last minute was he intercepted and impressed to keep quiet. Worst of all, the medical staff on base, including low level nurses, were shown the bodies.

Saul sensed in his superiors at Wright Field no panic or confusion, just urgent resolve to get this one right. No sloppy mistakes. He sensed the same resolve from the uniformed men arrayed around him, some of whom were part of that first crash recovery. The only one in the truck nonplussed by the situation—in fact he'd dozed most of the way—was a gentleman from Los Alamos National Lab. He was a senior scientist there presumably, but no one knew his name. He wore an expensive three-piece suit, so the soldiers referred to him as The Suit.

Once the trucks were parked, the soldiers hustled up the embankment to carry out their orders. They were not rough. Guns were out but not raised. They made clear their displeasure at finding so many civilians on the site. They asked their questions, conveyed their message, and escorted them back to their vehicles, standing watch until each one was down the road.

The police were interviewed together. The message was the same, but they were given a card with a phone number on it and a special task. If it ever came to their attention, after a week or a month or a year or ten years, that any of the civilians who were present today started running their mouths about it, call the number on the card and be ready to share that civilian's name. Both officers agreed. They were eager to help. The phone number was connected to the phone on Saul's desk back in Dayton.

Saul would have preferred to speak with the police himself, to form a bond with them that he could use later, but he kept to the perimeter while the interviews were happening. His injuries made him memorable, and he wanted to minimize the chance that one of these people would be able to recall him after the fact. He and The Suit walked along the tapered edge of the craft, their eyes collecting every detail. They did not speak. There was nothing yet to say.

Solon Brown was eager to get off the mesa after his chat with the soldiers. He turned onto 550 toward the Colorado line. He made it several miles before the trauma fully hit him. His arms were shaking too badly to keep hold of the wheel. He pulled over and staggered into the ditch, then kept on walking straight into the desert. He wept and prayed and shouted into the great blue sky for God to guide him. He stayed out there until the sun was low. When he finally forced himself to get back in the car, he ran his hands over the steering wheel, his day bag and lunch pail, his sermon notebooks. He felt his face in the mirror. All of it was unfamiliar, like he'd gotten into another man's car, inhabiting another man's body.

There were only three things Solon was certain of. His faith in Christ was unchanged. He would never think of life on this planet or its future in the same way again. If he tried to explain why, to share that knowledge, no one, absolutely no one, would ever believe him.

He turned the car around and drove toward home, uncertain of the man whose face his wife and children would search when he got there.

On the mesa, Saul and The Suit looked across the sloped surface of the craft. Saul's analytical mind stoically thrashed the puzzle before him while his index finger tapped the top of Bill Ferguson's Kodak that now hung around his neck. As with all his previous intel missions, he was confident, even at this late hour, that he would root out its secrets. The Roswell craft was torn to pieces, but the bodies were intact. This one had no damage at all, but the bodies were scorched somehow. Were these two random accidents, or a pattern? Was this intentional? An escalation? A message in a bottle? Enough.

Saul huffed and stepped onto the rim of the disc. The Suit tut-tutted this brash display but otherwise said nothing as Saul paced toward the apex.

The skin of the hull was perfectly smooth and clean, except for the tracks of dusty footprints from the oil men's boots. Saul noticed a series of evenly spaced, inlaid portholes. From an angle they appeared the same dull gray as the surrounding metal. When directly over them, the glass became reflective like a clouded mirror. If he crouched closer he could see through the glass into the interior chambers. One such porthole, which was encircled by many footprints, looked down on two more little bodies slumped over control panels. Saul pressed the camera lens close and snapped a picture.

Here he turned and began a wide circuit around the central dome. It bothered him that even as he was walking across it he had no idea what this was, and was becoming less certain with each step. His training forbade him from jumping to wild conclusions with so little solid information, but the scene before him was so impossible that wild conclusions were all he could reach for. This was, among other more severe anxieties, highly annoying to him. He felt trapped between two blinders that he could not see over the top of. The first blinder was his training as an intelligence analyst, which compelled him to categorize a thing until it made sense and then rank it on a scale of threat. Everything he had ever seen with his own eyes had made sense—even the unspeakably horrible things. It all followed the logic of men in the world. Not this. The second blinder was human intellect, which told him that impossible things are not real—they are askew reflections of something that is possible, that is real. These two impulses were closing in on him now. Staid intellect compelled Saul to believe there must be a rational explanation, but the analyst in him knew that the few facts he had did not fit any explanation. He felt like he'd been run into a box canyon. There was no way out—unless all of this could be made to disappear. He realized this is exactly what his superiors at Wright Field intended him to do.

He stomped his foot, partly out of frustration but partly to test the reality of what was beneath him. With a little nudge it might dissolve into dragon's breath and settle as dew upon the rocks... It did not. But something odd. He stomped again. His footfalls made no sound. It was as though his body had neither weight nor force. It was as though he was the thing that was unreal.

Nonsense. He needed more data, and Saul was determined to squeeze it out of this thing one way or the other.

Perhaps it was this burst of deep thought that caused him to notice a fuzziness in his head, a strange sensation almost like an electric current humming on the inside of his skull plate. He had gotten used to all sorts of odd phantom impressions from his injuries, but never like this. He could actually feel the mass of his own brain in relation to the gap between it and the plate. Electrical impulses leapt out of the thicket of a billion dendrites licking at the wall of forged metal. Signals trying to get out.

Saul decided he'd better get back on solid ground. As he turned, he noticed another porthole where he saw the form of another body. This one moved. He lowered himself to his knees for a closer look. On the other side, a face raised toward the glass. It looked almost human. Very carefully, Saul lifted the camera to his good eye, focused the lens and snapped a picture. The large black eyes blinked. Saul smirked.

"What now, smart guy?" he asked the creature. "Time to see what you're made of."

Very slowly and disjointed, in a voice that was not his own, these exact words were repeated back to him inside Saul's own head.

what now smart guy time to see what youre made of

It was the beginning of a conversation. One that would go on for a long, long time.

| 4 |

Constituent Services

I am a realist. That is my lane on the Hill. As a national security advisor to one of the Gang of Eight, let me assure you that realism is what they need. Because for every guy like me there are two more, plus the member usually, who are bleeding-heart idealists. These are folks who say let's fight the Taliban by building girls' schools in Afghanistan. Let's make sure the libraries in the madrasas receive a shipment of up-to-date science textbooks. Let's seed all of sub-Saharan Africa with solar-paneled easy-bake ovens. Make sure the boots on the ground have a weekly tea with the village elders and give out lollipops to the kiddies. Build hospitals and health clinics and train the staff. There is no end of ways to be helpful. During the War on Terror, in Iraq, the idealists loved to say that if you just drain the swamp all the mosquitoes will die. It's the perfect bullshit phrase because it allows you to believe that the mission objective is clear (it's not) and the follow-on operation will be straightforward (it won't). Draining the swamp, what that quaint phrase really means is sending a bunch of guys in to stomp out the bad parts of the culture you don't like—the people, systems, and practices. Draining the swamp is nothing at all like tromping over to the edge of the bog, kicking a hole in the beaver dam and letting gravity take care of the rest. Even if you succeed, and the culture dries out for a while, there could be a hundred reasons that swamp formed in that place, and you'll never figure out what they all are. It comes back. It seeps up through the ground. In places where people are killing one another—which, lest you take me for a chauvinist, is pretty much everywhere—they have been killing one another in much the same way for the much same reasons for hundreds of years, if not longer. I have seen this with my own eyes. Three tours in Iraq. I had more than my fill of tea with the Arab Methuselahs. I kicked in a lot of doors. I saw more than my share of MRAPs, packed with my buddies, popped by IEDs. When a suicide vest goes off, the body undergoes rapid disassembly. Because the neck is mostly soft tissue, the head usually shoots up like a champagne cork. If you are far enough away, and especially if the damn fool set it off before he meant to, it is the funniest thing you will ever see. The head falls straight down and lands with a crunch, all the little skull bones grinding together. The look of surprise on these faces. I am a realist.

The idealists are good people. I'm friends with them. We should all be glad to have them around. But they are always wrong. The reason for this is simple. It's not that their ideas do not help people on an individual basis. Many, many lives have been saved by their projects. But the ultimate goal, whatever it may be—stability, peace, social transformation—you can get 99% of the way and there will always be at least one guy waiting for you. He's got a bomb or a Kalashnikov, and a rabid distaste for change. He's there to drink your tears. He's there to lay waste to all your careful, thoughtful, helpful plans. And he's always right on time. This guy is why I am a realist.

I make this clear at the beginning so people don't assume I'm nothing more than a hard-hearted deficit hawk. I like people just fine and have no qualms with the species as a collective group. I don't care whatever magic number the funny money is set to at any given quarter. It's just that I know how the world works, and I cannot abide wasting effort operating contrary to its immutable rules. I'm allergic to delusions and I do not suffer starry-eyed fools.

There was only this one time when reality became so extreme that it outstripped my realism. The thing that I saw made fools of us all, and delusions were suddenly the only thing that made any sense. It damn near broke me.

The eight principals were briefed on the situation in the morning, no staff allowed in the SCIF. They decided to read in the national security aides, so we went down in the afternoon. We weren't to do anything. There was no job. The briefing was information only, so we would not be caught flatfooted if and when events took a turn. It was a Thursday, and all the members were flushing out to the airports heading home for the weekend.

The SCIF was located in the basement. Forgive me—the Sensitive Compartmented Information Facility. The Capitol has a way of rendering its employees incomprehensible to the general public. The SCIF is a regular conference room that has been sealed in various ways to keep the information shared within it from seeping out. A Capitol Police Officer is posted at the door for as long as the information is on site. For this briefing there were two, one on each side. Every electronic device short of a pacemaker must be removed and placed in a bin at the door. You can write down notes on these little pieces of paper, but the Security Director collects them before you leave. You can reference them again only inside of the SCIF. The information presented at this briefing was visual and not complicated. I did not need to take notes. The two briefers were from the Office of Naval Intelligence.

What else can I tell you?

This was in 2019, before the most recent wave of revelations, back when the members knew better than to ask questions they did not want to know the answer to. Most of them, anyway. This all started, of course, with that *New York Times* story that dropped just before Christmas 2017, the one that revealed the Pentagon had been running a secret UFO investigation unit secretly funded by three Senators who tucked $22 million into an appropriations bill—not in the 1960s but in 2007. That story provoked some chin scratching on the Hill. One effect of the existence of this office was that in 2014 the Navy put in place a formal reporting structure so that its aviators had a way to report these UFO-type objects they were beginning to see over their training ranges. Before this, it was all rumor, stories, folklore, cheesy movies. Now there were stories written down in official memoranda, paired with hard data, multi-sensor capture, some video, and more importantly, an information pipeline that rendered plausible deniability impossible. That put the bureaucrats at the end of the spigot in an impossible and over-exposed position. What if some of those official stories got out, what if some images leaked, and you were the last one holding the bag? What if you were the one paper-pusher who saw something but didn't say something? Like any smart mid-level bureaucrat, they tossed this hot potato up to their ultimate bosses. By 2018, the Armed Services and Intelligence Committees for the House and the Senate began receiving more regular and urgent briefings on these objects. I'm not suggesting this was thought out. The law of gravity dictates that crap flows downhill, but in Washington the bureaucratic imperative can make a turd roll up hill.

Still, in those first two years—2018 and 2019—very few members were aware this was happening. Only a handful were interested. Anyone could request a briefing and the boys in Naval Intelligence would have to trudge up the Hill and present their slide deck. Some of the members who requested briefings were the loons of the House. I got the sense some of them were doing it just for the entertainment value. The staff made no end of jokes about them. When my boss told me to submit a request for a personal briefing, I thought he was pranking me. When I realized he was serious, I begged him not to get involved. If word got out that he was asking to be briefed on UFOs, how would anyone take him seriously on national security matters or anything else? When the briefings were held, I found other places to be, and he was good enough not to require my attendance. I was not about to torch my reputation by being branded a UFO nut. That Thursday afternoon in the SCIF was the first time I had to take any of this seriously.

I have to be very careful about what I say now. As an employee of a Congressional committee, I had to sign a non-disclosure agreement. All it takes is one word that runs afoul of that agreement, a slip of the tongue. The first thing that would happen is that I would be fired. I would lose my security clearance. Two black marks that would make me unemployable. If they determined I burbled classified information, I might be arrested, and if I was arrested, I would go to jail. It is the most surreal high-wire act imaginable to be having a normal conversation with a person and know that the words in my mouth can upend every single piece of my life. So I have to be careful and speak slowly. I cannot reveal what I was shown in the SCIF. I cannot tell you what was said, who said what, or who said nothing at all. The regulations stipulate that staff 'shall not discuss either the substance or procedure of the work of the Committee with any person not a member of the Committee for any purpose.' That includes you and this purpose. You are the person the regs were written for.

It's funny—but this is also important to understand—the members of Congress are just as tied up as someone like me. They are not employees so there's no one to make them sign a non-disclosure agreement, though the Pentagon would do it in a heartbeat if they could think of a justification. Nor do they have security clearances due to the fact that they are constitutionally appointed officers of the government. Anyone whose title is mentioned in the Constitution, from the members of a jury up to the President, can be shown state secrets without the rigmarole of getting an approved security clearance. Very high minded. Very City on a Hill. But the Defense establishment and the Intelligence Community have a loophole. It's called need-to-know. Those officers can only be shown classified material if they need it to fulfill their particular government responsibilities. Who determines need-to-know? The bureaucrats who manage the classified material. I'm going to list some scenarios. These are based solely on things I've read on the internet. Imagine a UFO drops down from space, flutters through the atmosphere to settle on the ocean surface, and then disappears beneath the water, and its entire trajectory is tracked by radar and visual imagery. Who needs to know that? Imagine multiple craft crash in the multiple spots in the American southwest in, I don't know, the late 1940s, and are recovered by the Army. Who needs to know that? Imagine those craft then had pieces of them turned over to major aerospace companies so that they could be reverse engineered in a project that was funded by taxpayer dollars but remains inaccessible to those taxpayers or even members of Congress. Who needs to know that? Imagine those craft contained dead pilots who do not appear human, but decades later when their tissue was tested, it was revealed they contain human DNA. Who needs to know? Who *should* know?

It's not an easy question. Because if any of those scenarios, which I have read on the internet, are even partly real, then they outstrip any regulation, any law's power to manage the situation. The words *need* and *know* shed all comprehensible meaning. The signifying substance of all words simply dissolve upon contact with this problem. Maybe certain things have gone unsaid for so long because there is no way to say them...

We have no idea how out of our depth we really are. So we keep on doing the things we've always done, follow protocol, play office, stamp papers and rearrange the filing cabinets, look busy.

Anyway, the morning briefing to the Gang of Eight and the afternoon briefing to staff were both classified Top Secret *and* need-to-know. Why would there be a last-minute SCIF briefing added to the schedule just before a holiday weekend, hypothetically speaking? Because someone in one of the agencies determined that something was about to happen that Congress should know about. Maybe some highly sensitive information was leaked, or hacked, or stolen by espionage. Maybe none of that happened. Sometimes information gets lost in the shuffle, and there's a narrow window when it escapes classification. A cockup, an oversight. Maybe something slipped out of the zoo, let's say. I got the impression from the briefing that there was something loose in the wild, and that our bosses might be hearing about it from their constituents in the coming weeks, days, or hours.

The only thing I can report—the only thing I still truly own—are the feelings I experienced once I walked out of the SCIF.

The staff spilled out in the basement corridor. They all scattered, going to their bosses. We all avoided eye contact, saying nothing. I stayed behind, put my back against a pillar because my legs were jelly. I knew that if I moved at all I would start shaking like a leaf. I had a hard time getting air into my lungs.

There is not a word for the emotion I was feeling. Some cross between awe and rage and extreme stress and hilarity. And shock, no less intense than the kind that comes from the trauma of seeing someone's life ripped from their body. The sense that nothing will ever be the same after this one brief moment. We're going to need new words.

I thought about my father and wished I could call him. My father was a big sci-fi nerd. When I was a kid he would make me watch all the old movies with him, the ones he grew up on. *The Day the Earth Stood Still. Forbidden Planet. Plan 9 From Outer Space.* If you just focus on those three titles, they were interesting movies, particularly in how the filmmaker wanted the spacecraft to look. The classic 1950s flying saucer with the tapered, sloping discs pressed together and the dome on top. Simple, clean lines, sleek, shiny. If you get past the giggle factor, ignore the transparent wires suspending it from the film studio gantry, it is an enigmatic design, a cipher. I thought how cool it would be if he could see such a thing filmed in high-definition with modern cameras, darting in and out of clouds, swooping over the real world. He would know what to do.

Thinking of my father steadied my legs and I was able somehow to walk up the stairwell to the elevator bank. Up to the boss's office suite. Where I locked myself in the bathroom.

I had myself a good stress cry, silent stabbing breaths, tears, the works. I was thinking that when the public saw what I was shown in the SCIF, we would be in an unprecedented situation. It would blow up the world. It would end politics as we know it. It would reset the calendar of human events to Day Zero. Not only would it rewrite the history of the last hundred years, it would in a single blow shatter the credibility—the legitimacy—of every government institution, of all scientists and experts. It would scare the living daylights out of every man, woman and child. Destabilization on an unimaginable scale. And remember, being a realist, I know that people don't like change and it only takes one of them.

The weight of this thing dropped square on my back. My boss would be at the podium trying to calm people down. The words he would have to use would be the most important words he'd ever had to speak. Now, I'm not the wordsmith in this shop. My role as national security advisor is to clarify the stakes, put the situation in context, so that the member can stake out a clear position and course of action, and then explicate to the public what is going on and what needs to be done. In this situation, not one of those was possible. The stakes were incomprehensible. There was no context. No one knew what was happening or what to do. There were no words.

After some time had passed I became sensible to a soft knocking on the bathroom door, someone checking on me. I thought everyone had left. I cleaned myself up and came out, mortified to see my boss standing there in the corridor holding a glass of scotch. He put it in my hand. In the other room, I saw the Majority Leader and the chairmen for Intelligence and Armed Services, House side. They were drinking too. Usually pols like these just play frenemies on TV. Not these two. They legitimately hate one another's guts. But they did not seem mad. They did not seem like anything, sipping away—the truce of a wake.

The boss could tell I was wrecked. He told me to catch a flight to the district. I could stay in his pool house, and we would hit the links on Saturday at his club. Take our minds off work, he said, cool as a cucumber.

On Friday afternoon I found myself sitting in the district office, outside of a conference room where the mayor was getting his periodic bout of face time. The boss is serious about constituent services.

The office is in a part of town that we're now supposed to call an underserved community. It's in a narrow, single-hallway, one-story school that was built in the '70s, wedged between two other buildings on the block, so no windows. Just a series of cinder block cells in a riot-proof bunker. Lucky for the kids the school closed years ago, and the outreach office occupies one large rectangular room in the front of the building with a tiny enclosed conference room. There are three rows of cubicles, and a waiting area with a playpen for the kiddies. It was only me and the woman answering phones, while the boss and the mayor were shooting the breeze in the conference room.

I was still on edge. Nothing had happened, but the call could come at any minute. I was beginning to think that was the real reason I was there. Nothing to do but wait. So I listened to the problems of the people who called into the office, to calm my nerves. I could only hear the cubicle lady's side of the conversation. The things she said into that phone, I will never forget. Not because the problems the callers relayed were particularly memorable. I'm sure she takes calls like these every day of the week. It's just that I was in a state of shock, hyperalert, and everything about that day flowed straight into long-term memory. She had a kind, even tone, listening patiently while they rambled, slipping in her interjections like a nurse who knows right where to place the needle so it doesn't pinch. Her hand never stopped jotting crisp notes on a legal pad.

...so you're still worried about your son... He's fifteen now... Summer's coming, do you have a plan?... Of course, oh I know, I see them there every morning, I pass that corner on my way to work... School lets out June 25th, a Tuesday... Is he in summer school? No, he passed all his classes... Oh I know, he's very bright... And Ronald is a small fry, if you don't mind me saying... The gangs, they tend to recruit the biggest boys and the smallest boys. I don't know why, maybe because they feel that the little guys are more susceptible to the message that they need protection, that they can be strong... Right, right, I remember Sabree. We tried so hard with him... Ma'am, I'm not a social worker. All I can tell you is what I would tell my sister. You need to get him something to do during the day. And I don't think movie passes every day is going to cut it. I'm going to give you two phone numbers. Do you have a pen ready?... The first one is Job Corps, it is a youth employment program. The mayor runs it out of his own office.... I know, he's wonderful. He's right here in fact, meeting with the Congressman... I will tell him... The second, well it's new to the city. It's kind of like a summer camp where the kids take

classes in the morning and learn baseball in the afternoon. ...Oh we give you a tuition voucher. You do have to pick it up here to sign for it. How does that sound?... Ok, let me know when you are ready.

That call with Ms. Russell was in progress when I sat down in the folding chair. The next call came immediately after.

Oh hi, Ms. Kinsington, nice to talk to you again... Yes you just caught me. How's your daughter's asthma? Better?... Ok, ok... How long has that been going on?... Since February, when we had that big rain?... And what has the landlord said about it?... This was the kitchen sink, you said?... That sounds awful... It's not a gas smell, correct, more like a sewer smell... Before I forget, I'm just going to make a note to mail you a carbon monoxide detector. That won't help with this, but they're good to have. Remember, you have to plug into a wall outlet. I keep mine in the outlet right beside my bed... I understand you want to file a complaint, I can help you place that... Your landlord is already on our list... Ms. Kinsington, I don't mean to cut you off, but I want to strongly discourage you from doing that... I know, I know... It's just that, you don't want to do anything that will help him build a case for an eviction notice. You want to help us build the case against him... I'm going to connect you with the housing authority, a nice lady there named Brenda Santos, she's the one to talk to... And don't forget about the free asthma clinic at the health center, two Saturdays from now. There will be a clown, balloons, games, things like that. Bring your daughter... Ok, have a nice weekend. Goodbye now.

The blinking lights on her phone panel went dark.

"Saving two lives, not bad for a day's work," I said.

This startled her as she thought she was alone. She swung around.

"I'm just a connector," she said without an ounce of self-satisfaction. "We connect them with social services, local or federal. Of course they like to talk to you. I tell them, I'm not a social worker, I can only say to you what I would say to my own sister if she were in that situation."

"Do you ever get discouraged?"

"No. Like the boss says, it's a game of inches. There are people like me, working for different organizations, taking calls all over the city.

We help a lot of people on an individual basis. Whether that's making things better overall, I don't know. It keeps things from getting worse, which is a win in my book."

Another realist.

The mayor left. The boss took a quick call on his cell. When he came out he went straight to the lady's cubicle. "Margaret," he said, "anything interesting?"

"The usual," she said.

He picked up the legal pad and leafed through several pages. While he did so, the phone rang, which Margaret diligently answered. Her demeanor on this call was totally different—still the big sister, but like she'd gotten a prank call from her kid brother. She hit the mute button. "Fox Mulder on line two," she said. I didn't get the joke, but the boss apparently did. He asked her to hand over the phone. She refused. He tried to grab it. She wrestled it away from him—playfully, but with forceful intent. She did not want him talking to this guy. When he'd had enough, he just opened his palm and she relented.

While they spoke, Margaret rolled her chair all the way back against the wall. "He calls every day without fail. And emails. Both. He thinks aliens landed in their UFOs back in the 1940s in all these places, and that the Army captured them and had been trying to reverse-engineer the technology. And that the Pentagon is keeping alien bodies in a freezer somewhere. I've gotten a real education. He wants the government to release all its evidence. Real tin foil hat type stuff. We don't have any wraparound services for that." She laughed at her joke.

"No, I have not seen any video," the boss said while shooting me a summoning eye.

Just like that I was plunged into the biggest crisis of my career—over the most absurd thing imaginable, while stuck in this ridiculous, windowless office.

"Why don't you post it on my Facebook page, and I'll take a look… It's already there? Good."

I wiped out my phone and there it was.

The panic lifted. I was in planning mode now. First step was to get Margaret out of there. I had to somehow create a secure place for us to be for the next few minutes or hours. Then I had to arrange travel back to Washington. He would want a statement prepped, and since we could not bring comms people in, that would fall to me.

I looked up at the boss, who was, as usual, cool as a cucumber. I must have looked more panicked than I realized because he put his hand on my shoulder and left it there.

"Do I think it's real? Well, people can make videos look like anything is real these days. The more important question is what do you believe?... And if it is in fact real, if it is otherworldly, we will have internal controls in place to protect us and to engage, in the event that that happens, in a healthy and safe way."

As soon as I heard it I grabbed the lady's notepad and wrote it down. That was the perfect statement. Anodyne, boring, paternalistic, calming. What can I say, the boss is a natural.

"If you learn anything, message me on Facebook. I will be monitoring the situation there. Ok... Thanks for calling, Robert. Good bye now."

He politely ushered out the phone lady, bidding her to enjoy her weekend, and then closed the door. He held up his phone, where the video clip was playing on loop. With that toothy, game-show host smile, he tried to soothe me.

"This big moment you've been shitting your pants over, when it comes, it won't play out like this. When that day comes, and it will, it's going to be personal for people. The moment will meet every person where they are at, and they will process it in their own way. And you're going to be amazed how fast normalcy will clap back. Will it blow everyone's minds? Sure will. But Ms. Russell is still going to be worrying about her son. And Ms. Kinsington is still going to be fighting her slum lord while trying to get asthma medication for her daughter. Politicians, we have a bad rap, but we get people. Even those of us who have never given two thoughts to UFOs will instinctively know what to do. Your side of the shop is going to play less a part in this than you realize. So cheer up. What do I always say: you worry too much."

That was it. We played some golf. I had a very good ribeye. All in all, a relaxing weekend.

The boss is a good man. I love the guy. But he is always fucking wrong.

This is not a problem that can be managed.

When little Ronald Russel gets lost to the streets, mom's not going to call in complaining about the gangs. She's going to think he was beamed up into a flying saucer. Ms. Kinsington is going to think that the sour smell wafting out of her drainpipes is caused by an army of little green men amassing in the sewers. Those will be the sane responses. Over 170,000 people live in 24-hour mental health institutions. Pity the poor nurse who breaks the news to them. Eight million Americans suffer from serious psychological disorders. What happens when they find out? What about the millions more barely hanging on by a thread. All it takes is one to lose their shit and do serious damage, and there will be more than one.

Religion? You still hear people worrying about how the faithful will react, but the bible thumpers will be a cakewalk compared to their competition. There are boatloads more rubes and hoopleheads taking their cues from the likes of Alex Jones and the manscaped minions on YouTube than there are churchgoers taking in a Sunday sermon. Before this is over, you're going to wish they had a pastor to talk sense into them. Going online will be like snorting QAnon and meth. The hoaxsters and the scammers will darken the skies like flying monkeys over Oz. The elderly will be plagued by ceaseless scam calls day and night hawking alien-invasion insurance that will take an act of Congress to put a stop to, but of course Washington will be far too busy to ever get to that. The Silicon Valley tech bros will want their piece of the action, naturally, and they will pour jug after jug of their special brand of unfiltered bullshit into the algorithms trying to get it.

The economy? Not my wheelhouse. Government, however, will grind to a halt. Politics will incinerate into a little pile of nuclear ash, which is why no politician with any sense and a little power, and especially no President, is going to want to touch this with a ten-foot pole—but that's not my concern.

The national security state is entirely dependent on the populace giving the practitioners of national power the benefit of the doubt. The public needs to believe that their government is managed by a revolving claque of ambitious but bumbling bureaucrats, people who at least feign an interest in doing the right thing. Above all, our managers need to be seen as operating from a default position of general incompetence, not as jackboots so ruthless and efficient as to pull off a global, decades-long project to keep fundamental truths of nature and science buried in secrecy. Without that comforting illusion, you cannot have a democracy and a national security state. And America must have a national security state.

I am a realist, remember, hence my dilemma.

Some of these fools in Congress think we've evolved past all that. The Cold War is over, they say. Disclosure and transparency is the way of the future. They're laying plans, drafting legislation. They'll spend ten years at least bogged down in classification law, trying to untangle the mess of authorities. It's a game of inches. But the future is all sunshine. Truth, justice, a chicken in every pot, and a flying car in every driveway. They will get right to the end zone—where you and I will be waiting for them. We're the guys in suicide vests who show up in what you think is the end of the story.

What's the ordinance of choice? Funny you should ask. Always have total situational awareness of the battlefield on which you are operating. The kind of bomb I'm talking about is packed with disinformation, little shards of truthiness, comforting pablum that will lull everyone back to sleep. A bullshit bomb. Just the sort of bomb someone in your line of work knows how to wire, plant, and detonate, Mr. Chief National Security Correspondent for the Newspaper of Record.

There are three threads you need to get a firm grasp on right now.

One. Only fools trust what they find on the internet. Don't be a fool. That's the message of your lighthearted puff piece on the video in question.

Is it real? Keep up. It doesn't matter if it's real or not. Draw a little official attention to it. Chum the waters in all the right corners of the internet and let the wingnuts tear themselves to pieces over it. DoD won't comment, of course. Everyone else throws up their hands, if they notice at all.

Two. Drones and balloons, on repeat. There is a troubling rash of drone incursions over secure military installations. I can point you to two recent incidents of a rival power conducting aerial surveillance with unknown cutting-edge technology. I can get you sources, currently serving Pentagon officials, off the record. The other side of this is that commercial drone technology has evolved to the point where there are drones that can look like anything, a cube, a sphere, a flying saucer. There are advanced, state-of-the-art technologies out there today that can maneuver, and flight controls that don't have control surfaces, that don't leave a trail, and they are being commercialized. Some of it belongs to our military, some of it is foreign adversaries, some of it is the drug cartels on the border, some of it is hobbyists. As for balloons, 10,000 are released every day over the United States. There is a lot of garbage in the sky.

Three. DoD and the Intelligence Community would love nothing more than to explain all of this to the American people, truly. Trouble is, much of the information about these apparent anomalous technologies remains classified. Some in Congress have been read in on some of it, many have not. Nobody wants for China to know that their advanced spy technology has been detected. Nobody wants to reveal our countermeasures. But such official secrecy comes at a cost, allowing conspiracy theories about government coverups to thrive unchecked. It's a terrible predicament, but their hands are tied. That should be a direct quote.

Weave these three threads through every article you write on the subject.

What's the truth? Indeed, the picture is rather blurry now, isn't it? Stitch these half-truths together a certain way and they form a whole truth, a version of it anyway. One truth is just as good as the other, and some are decidedly better. Some truths are too dangerous to be let out in the first place. Our truth at least sounds like common sense. The more mysterious and mystical the answer appears to be, the easier it is to dispense with. People in general have a low tolerance for ambiguity. Everyone's busy. Everyone keeps on scrolling. Life goes on and then you die.

Will it work? Anyone who clings to one version of reality, it can be taken away, and they will acclimate to the new reality in short order. We are knowledge terrorists. We take their truth and blow it to smithereens. Obliterated. Erased. And the best part is, when our bomb goes off, no one will even know it happened. We will have swapped out one reality for another, and none of them will be the wiser. They'll be living in our world, the real world, with not a thought in their head that it could have been any other way.

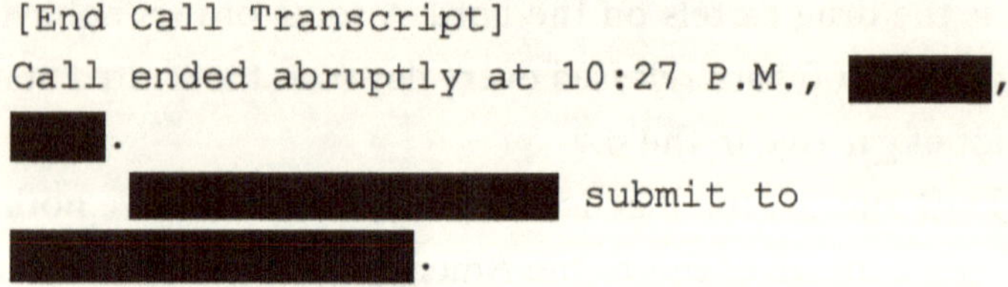

| 5 |

Author's Note

Ray Bradbury wrote *The Martian Chronicles* in 1950 as a collection of short stories that knit together to tell a sprawling story about humanity emigrating from their ruined planet to Mars. The Martians were beside the point, if they even show up at all (read it for yourself). Bradbury was much more interested in how it would impact society and human nature if we could simply leap off planet Earth in rockets and settle on an alien world. This is after all why most writers of science-fiction bother to dwell on these strange ideas—as a pretext for unmasking the strangeness that is in us.

If beings from another world really exist, and if we ever get to learn that they have been visiting us in their UFOs, (two mind-bending prospects that I find increasingly likely), then all of us will find ourselves on a planet—Earth—that is far different than the one we'd thought we'd been living on all this time. What will that be like? How will we view ourselves and our history—not just through their eyes, if they have eyes—but from the vantage of our own newly acquired knowledge? How will the revelation of this enormous secret interact with our institutions, our politics, and our shared history? How did we get to this point, and what is yet to come? The four short stories in this collection were written with these questions in mind.

My interest in UFOs was piqued by the December 16, 2017 *New York Times* article, *Glowing Auras and 'Black Money': The Pentagon's Mysterious U.F.O. Program*, by Helene Cooper, Ralph Blumenthal, and

Leslie Kean. A growing number of members of Congress, particularly on the Armed Services and Intelligence committees spent 2018 and 2019 studying military encounters with UFOs, which they rebranded with the more politically palatable term Unidentified Aerial Phenomenon. In the summer of 2020, these UFO-curious legislators inserted a provision into the Intelligence Authorization Act for Fiscal Year 2021 that required the Director of National Intelligence to submit a public report synthesizing all the data the military and Intelligence Community had collected on UAP. The act was signed into law December 27, 2020, which started a countdown of 180 days until the report was to be released. Despite the many other breaking news events in early 2021—the COVID pandemic, President Trump's Stop the Steal campaign and the January 6 insurrection, the Biden Administration transition—there was a palpable sense of anticipation among the public and the media over just what secrets the government was about to reveal about UFOs.

To someone like me, who never considered that the UFO stories told and retold over the decades could be true, this was a disorienting moment. Writing is my preferred way of processing something that I do not understand. I began writing articles and blog posts about UFOs in May 2021, mainly tracking (and trying to make sense of) public statements and actions made about UFOs by our political leaders and executive branch bureaucrats. In June, the Office of the Director of National Intelligence released its report, titled *Preliminary Assessment: Unidentified Aerial Phenomenon*. It did not say UFOs were real, but it did say that the government had collected recent evidence that UAP "demonstrates breakthrough aerospace capabilities," with flight characteristics that include the ability "to remain stationary in winds aloft, move against the wind, maneuver abruptly, or move at considerable speed, without discernable means of propulsion." At this point, after the possibility of UFO reality had been percolating for over three years, I became convinced that the simple story of UFOs as myth and misidentification was not the full story.

It is always a bad idea for a writer to explain his work, and I will not do that here. However, as these four short stories are the products of a specific moment in time (i.e., the U.S. government's sudden public interest in UFOs circa 2021-2024), and as they may one day be of use as primary historical sources in their own right, I feel compelled to explicate some of the real events and atmospherics that inspired them.

The first story, *Bucket of Piss*, was written in the summer of 2021 (completed September 2021). Among other themes, I wanted to explore how the old adage about a UFO landing on the White House lawn would interact with our political reality in non-straightforward ways. The nonplussed disinterest and put-upon annoyance of some of the political and military characters—that UFOs, even if real, represent a distraction from things that are more important—are an underappreciated factor in why UFO disclosure has taken so long to come about. Conversely, the chief-of-staff character, who quotes real UFO history chapter and verse, is also drawn from real life examples of government employees who care deeply about this issue, such as John Podesta, chief-of-staff to President Clinton, and a senior advisor to both Presidents Obama and Biden.

Ubuntu was written during the first half of 2022 (completed July 2022). No one knows what UFOs actually are, and ufologists do not agree on any one theory. The Extraterrestrial Hypothesis is the most popular, but there are others, including trans-dimensional beings, a hidden Earth-based civilization known as ultraterrestrials, and representations from the fairy world. Another idea that came into vogue in these years is that UFOs are sent by humans from the future. Award-winning investigative reporter Ross Coulthart began to exclusively focus his reporting on UFOs with the publication of his 2021 book *In Plain Sight*. During interviews in 2022, he began to mention that some of his highly placed unnamed sources were telling him that UFOs were piloted by future humans, and that the reason for extreme government secrecy about UFOs is that public disclosure would endanger the time-travelers' plans to stop an impending global cataclysm. Whoever told Coulthart this, they were not just talking to one UFO journalist. In May 2022, Congressman Mike Gallagher, who then sat on the House Armed Services Committee and the Intelligence Committee, said this in an interview:

"The third really interesting one is that it's inter-dimensional, that it's us from the future. ... People of the future have figured out how to bend space and time. ... I would say there is a group of people on the outside who believe this is more plausible than the extraterrestrial explanation, serious people too."

Whether any of that is true is anyone's guess. *Ubuntu* imagines how such a time travel mission would work if it were true.

Four Conversations was written in 2023 (completed November 2023). The four sections of this story depict four distinct eras of UFO history: the late 1940s, the 1960s, the 1980s, and a post-disclosure world in our near future. Each vignette is speculative, however the details of the UFO crash in Aztec, New Mexico, including all of the named witnesses (with the exception of Saul and The Suit) are as close to the historical truth of the event as we currently understand it. Scott and Suzanne Ramsey did painstaking, years-long research to prove that those events actually occurred. I drew many details about what happened on the mesa from their 2016 book *The Aztec UFO Incident.*

Constituent Services was written from the fall of 2023 through the spring of 2024 (completed May 2024). The genesis of this story came from an article by my friend Chris Sharp, founder and chief writer of the UFO news page *Liberation Times,* which he founded in 2021, and for which I contributed articles in 2022. Sharp had a source on Capitol Hill who told him of a congressional staffer who was presented with evidence of UFOs in a SCIF briefing and had their entire worldview shaken as a result. None of the characters in *Constituent Services* are meant to represent any real-life people. However, several of the quotes from my first-person narrator are modified direct quotes from actual public figures, which I have sourced below.

Congressman Andre Carson sits on the House Intelligence Committee. As chairman of the Subcommittee on Counterterrorism,

Counterintelligence and Counterproliferation, he held the first congressional hearing on UFOs in fifty years, which took place May 17, 2022. Carson's public statements reveal that he has been thinking deeply about the challenge of preparing the public for UFO disclosure. In January 2022, the advocacy group End UAP Secrecy released this clip of Carson:

"If it is otherworldly we will have internal controls in place to protect us and to engage, in the event that that happens, in a healthy and safe way."

In May 2023, Carson said this in an on-camera interview with documentarian James Fox:

"Are people ready for some kind of revelation that deals with extraterrestrial life, life that is interdimensional, life that is otherworldly? And so that kind of revelation unearths people's beliefs, their religious beliefs, their spiritual beliefs that they've been taught all their lives. And so, if such a revelation were to present itself, how does it get presented, and can it be done in a way that people are accepting of it?"

Dr. Sean Kirkpatrick was the founding director of the All-Domain Anomaly Resolution Office (AARO), which Congress mandated the IC/DoD stand up in order to study UAP. He served as director from May 2022 through December 2023, and he consistently maintained that the U.S. government had no evidence of UFOs or a UFO coverup. During a panel discussion on November 7, 2023 at The Hayden Center, George Mason University, titled "UAP - The Search for Clarity," Kirkpatrick said the following:

"All of the evidence we have, and all of the observations we have, including the ones where people say 'I don't understand it. It looks like it's violating the laws of physics'—I guarantee you it's not. There is advanced state-of-the-art technologies out there today that can maneuver, and flight controls that don't have control surfaces, that don't leave a trail, and they are being commercialized."

Julian E. Barnes covers national security for *The New York Times.* In an October 28, 2022 article headlined, *Many Military U.F.O. Reports Are Just Foreign Spying or Airborne Trash,* Barnes wrote the following:

"Much of the information about the unidentified phenomena remains classified. While Congress has been briefed on some of the conclusions about foreign surveillance, Pentagon officials have kept most of the work secret — in large measure because they do not want China or other countries to know that their efforts to spy on the American military were detected. But such official secrecy comes at a cost, allowing conspiracy theories about government lies to thrive unchecked."

Barnes's sources were an unspecified number of "American officials [who] spoke on the condition of anonymity to discuss the classified work."

In *Constituent Services* the national security advisor and the journalist enter into a pact to foist a UFO disinformation campaign on the public. In reality, the extraordinary implications of UFOs and the slipperiness of the evidence makes it easy to convince people of the balloon/drone/misidentification theory without having to resort to disinformation. I am not suggesting that Kirkpatrick and Barnes were consciously lying in 2022 and 2023. There is no evidence that can prove that. I am suggesting that both men swallowed a single, simple story of UFOs, and for personal and professional reasons chose to use their platforms to perpetuate that story. They were not alone in doing so.

But somewhere down the chain of custody of classified government UFO secrets, someone—several someones—decided to lie. It was a fateful turning point in human history. Excavating the details of that decision, and making sense of it, will be the job of writers and historians for years to come. The four stories in this collection represent my own meager attempts in these first years of UFO disclosure.

—JS

May 27, 2024

West Orange, New Jersey